Shaf
and the
Remington

"A vivid chronicle of life in a small corner of Europe opens onto an exploration of history from the Byzantines to the Ottomans to the Second World War. This is a gripping, exuberantly written tale, mixing genres and vocabularies, tracking the elusive dream of interethnic harmony. Rana Bose's story is beautiful and wise." Sherry Simon, Canada Chair in Translation and Cultural History, Director of Concordia's Interdisciplinary PhD in Humanities Program, author of *The City in Translation: "Urban Cultures of Central Europe.*"

"In his new novel *Shaf and the Remington*, Rana Bose paints complex, unforgettable characters that last long after the book is read. In an epistolary style, Ben, and his tutor, Shaf, narrate events that changed their lives and the history of nations. Bose forces us to face our own anger, animosity, arrogance, and religious and racial intolerance. Masterfully crafted, the final pages of the book compel the reader to start over again." Nilambri Ghai, founding member and editor of *Montréal Serai*, author of From Johanne to Janaki: *Bringing Vikings to Varanasi.*

"Set in the fictitious town of Sabzic in what is clearly Yugoslavia but never identified as such, Bose relates the personal stories of Ben and Shaf against the backdrop of invading panzer divisions and local partisans. But this is in no way historical fiction. Rather, it is an allegory to the forces of human nature, which pit the petty desire to divide against the will to unite. ... [Rana Bose] would certainly merit a place in Canada's pantheon of outstanding writers." Ian Thomas Shaw, *The Ottawa Review of Books.*

Rana Bose

Shaf
and the
Remington

Baraka
Books

Montréal

© Rana Bose
ISBN 978-1-77186-295-0 pbk; 978-1-77186-306-3 Epub;
978-1-77186-307-0 pdf

Cover by Vincent Partel
Book Design by Folio Infographie
Editing and proofreading by Blossom Thom, Anne Marie Marko and Robin Philpot

Legal Deposit, 3rd quarter 2022
Bibliothèque et Archives nationales du Québec
Library and Archives Canada

Published by Baraka Books of Montreal

Printed and bound in Quebec

Trade Distribution & Returns
Canada – UTP Distribution: UTPdistribution.com

United States
Independent Publishers Group: IPGbook.com

We acknowledge the support from the Société de développement des entreprises culturelles (SODEC) and the Government of Quebec tax credit for book publishing administered by SODEC.

Société
de développement
des entreprises
culturelles
Québec

Funded by the Government of Canada
Financé par le gouvernement du Canada | Canada

The carpet looks wonderful, but if you bring your nose closer, it smells.

-Overheard in a café

- for Josephine Chameli, Colette Daisy and Fran Amiya

Section One

Ben and the Town That Diedar Built

Chapter One

I made a swift U-turn and parked my rental car about twenty-five metres away from the house with the big arched double wooden doors. I cut the engine of the car and it coughed to a boisterous stop. The watch said it was eight thirty-one.

I rolled down the window. The moldy and fusty smell of the canal water swept over the painted parapet, crossed the street, rose up into the air above it and then went straight for my nostrils. I stiffened my grip on the steering wheel, overwhelmed by the staleness that suddenly invaded the car. In the distance I saw the shimmering amber reflections of the canal water under the arch of the stone bridge; on the Strand, electric lights had replaced many of the old gas lamps from the previous century. The large slabs of rock on the walkway under the bridge glistened, like a fresh downpour had just happened. But it had been like that for the past several centuries. Horseshoes had honed down the rocks into smooth, shiny undulations, and even on a dry sunny day, it seemed like the canal had just overflowed or a sudden downpour had left a pock-marked reminder of the Sultans and Dukes who rode down the Strand and the walkways of this centuries-old town.

For several thousand years, horses had been domesticated in the high grasslands up in the northeast of our country. For the last six centuries, majestic stallions had been ridden-in by marauding adventurers ready to occupy, loot, convert, decimate and sometimes revive forgotten lifestyles. Horses had been their head-bobbing accomplices. The cobblestones bore this imprint and the buildings, the walls, the bridges, the canals bore the changing stamp of succeeding empires, in the facades of the houses, in the colours of the tiles on the domes and the tapestries inside the places of worship. Invasion after invasion and the assimilation that followed, for a few centuries at a time, bore testimony to the tempest that this region had witnessed. But for now, there was stillness and anxiety as I focused on the house, after having driven for more than ten hours.

From where I was parked, I could see the target address, the road in front, the stone bridge, the Strand under the bridge, and a little to the left and on the opposite side of it, lay the other part of town where I would go occasionally, while growing up. I could see the house lights in the distance, the blue grey shadows of the mountains which spread like a blanket, that had been thrown casually on the horizon. And as I looked into the darkness, I could hear the faint sound of a horse carriage crossing over on the stone bridge, as I had heard and seen some forty years ago.

***

His name is Shaf. I have not seen him since the end of the War, which was about forty years ago. He was my tutor till the end. His knowledge of Physics and Algebra was immaculate. Spotless, that is. But the Philosophy that he associated with his understanding of forces, the laws of motion and gravity, could be elusive and refract minds away from the obvious. And that is what attracted me to him, his ability to point out what is beyond the obvious—under the skin and beyond the horizon—something that you did not see or feel while you were staring at it. Maddening, insanely provocative were his ways of highlighting phenomena and behaviours which were beyond the tangible.

He was always poorly shaved, but there was no attempt to grow a beard as such. Some dark brown stubble grew in a haphazard manner. His eyes were light brown, and his hair had blond streaks, here and there. His nose was unusual in that he had a raised bridge roughly one quarter inch below where his eyebrows nearly met ready for glasses, but he never wore any. And beyond that it was like a ski-slope coming down at a seventy-degree angle, followed by a gentle flare into nostrils that were noticeably hairless. When he smiled, occasionally, his teeth were barely visible, because his upper lip was significantly well endowed, compared to the lower one. His cheek bones were unobtrusive, like his character. He often wore a beret, that was pulled to one side. He rode a bicycle in a wavering, unsure manner like he would change direction any moment; but I learnt later that it was perhaps a deceptive ploy. Either that or he was distracted and reckless.

***

I sensed a movement behind me, shadowy and dubious; but there were no shadows as such, just a feeling, as no one was standing by, or waiting in silence. Nothing was visible in the side-view mirror. No one approached the door of the big mansion. My quixotic imagination required that I would see a dark silhouette appear from nowhere or, at least, on top of the stone bridge looking down. Absolutely nothing happened. And yet, there was a sulking presence that had taken the form of the smell that lurked under the arches. When I looked into the rear-view mirror, I saw the road curve behind me, sharply, as if I was forbidden to look behind. There were no cars behind either. If a curfew had been declared, I would have known for sure, but the stillness was reminiscent. I remembered to turn off all of the car lights. I kept looking across at the massive wooden doors. That was the address I had been given. The bone-penetrating cold crept in through the partially open window, as if querying the fluids in my marrow. I felt icicles were entering and exiting my body—and while I held on to the deceptive warmth inside a rapidly cooling car, there was no choice but to put my gloves on and lift the jacket collar around my face. I stared deep into the shimmering waters of the canal and remembered my inglorious grandfather salivating about it as a wild and prodigious river, that was full of leaping and cavorting trout.

Well, yes, several kilometres upstream, the canal was actually a river. With fish, boats, piers and daredevil kids doing cannonball leaps, in summer. But here, in the town, as the river became a canal, the currents changed, the fish were gone and only a few tourist-trapping gondola-style boats lazed by once in a while. And there was the pale-yellow facade on all the houses, that peered through the patches of green foliage, as one went a little way onto the top of the mountain and looked down at the city. The green canal, circled around the city, with the stone bridge above it. In the distance, you could see the church spires projecting out, through the foliage. If you looked even more carefully, you would see mosques—not so ubiquitous as when I was growing up here, with their domes and single minarets to the side—and as you looked even more carefully you would occasionally see a building with a Byzantine flair, which could be a synagogue or an Orthodox church. I had not been back in the town for several years.

The mansion was five floors high. There were two wrought-iron fenced-in patches of green on either side of the doors, which had been placed right in the middle of the building. The shrubs were not well maintained and yet provided a sense of order. Two lamps on either side of the moulded cement frame, that held the door, lit up both patches of green, evenly. The two doors could very well be called gates. There were brass plates, studs and knobs all over them. The moulded and elaborate cement arch over the door encased a stained-glass arrangement, shaped like a school geometry compass. The doors were obsequiously large. A horse-drawn carriage could perhaps go through this opening, and possibly did, several decades ago. There were two marble steps in front of them. Not much height if the canal overflowed.

A big car appeared from nowhere, lurched to a stop in front of me, backed up and parked like a dolt, and the engine was left to idle. I watched the car. It was four minutes past nine. I had been instructed by the Serf to wait outside between 8:30 p.m. and 9:15 p.m. Nobody seemed to be getting out of the car. The double doors opened and a lady in a pair of jeans and red shirt with a black scarf and a bomber jacket walked out briskly, stopping to light a cigarette, and then she powered down the street.

Simultaneously thereafter two things happened.

A man in a dark suit, shirt collar open and tie loose, got out of the car in front and staggered his way across the street to the big house. He was fortunate that no cars were passing by because he had stopped in the middle of the street to pull out a pocket watch to check the time. No cares. He managed to waddle across the street towards the double doors. He had just about pulled out his keys, when I heard a splash on the left-hand side, right next to the canal and the wall that bordered it; the lights under the bridge were bright and first I saw two hands and then a head emerging from below the parapet. A wild persona, hair tousled, reddish brown and grey, long beard, clothes wet, even some mossy, dark green weed fell away from his shoulders, as he rolled over. He had been waiting for the car.

The man from the car was now focused zealously on the keyhole on the big door and then he opened it with excessive force, slipping a bit in the process and finally managing to lurch in. Immediately, the man who had emerged from the canal, vaulted over the parapet, raced across like a rolling wet bush, timing his crossing, so that he would be able to grab the big door before it would close, slowly. The squelch from his sneakers would have been heard across the canal, gone over the bridge and into the mountains in the distance and into the decades left behind.

The door hydraulics allowed a five-second interval, before it started to move towards closure. He grabbed the handle and waited for a few seconds. I did not waste time. I jumped out of my car and followed the two of them. I knew I had to get into the mansion. This was very clearly outlined to me, as a time-bound sequence of events that I must avail myself of. I waited for canal-man to enter, and caught a fleeting glimpse of the inebriated fellow entering the elevator situated at the far end of the chandelier-lit, fully marbled hallway. I pretended to walk away casually, but whipped around and grabbed the door handle as well, before the door would start moving back. I entered behind canal-man. The inebriated fellow was already on his way up. The door closed slowly behind me. I waited as canal-man squelched his way down a corridor to the left, leaving a trail of water, mud and mossy weeds across the immaculately swept hallway. He entered the last door at the end and went down the stairs. I followed at a distance, with my noiseless sneakers emitting neither a squeak nor a squelch. I doubted if the canal-man followed this stealthy sequence every night, carrying moss, water and mud, as he squelched his way in.

He went for the boiler room at the end, opened a hatch door, and went in with a superbly timed diving cum crawling motion. The door remained unlatched, as he walked away, swinging a bit. I waited a while and then pushed the hatch door open and attempted to imitate his movement, with less finesse. It was 9:30 p.m.

It was dark inside. I saw he was taking his clothes off at the far end in a dimly lit corner and hanging them up on a nylon cord he had strung up across the room. His shoulders glistened as he dried himself with what looked like a greasy towel and then he went over to a sink and washed his hands up to his elbows and then his feet, up to his knees. He stood a few moments in front of a hand-held mirror that he had hung up over the sink and I ducked out of the way so he would not catch me in the reflection. I was still about twenty feet away from him, behind a pillar.

He then pulled out a pajama from a small suitcase, along with a singlet. He was chanting a tune, in a language I hardly understood. Finally, he went across to another wall in the dark boiler room and came back with a skull cap on, and a small rug in his hand. He laid the rug down, at

19

an oblique angle on the floor. I noted that the shape of the rug had been marked up on the cement floor, with a chalk outline. I could barely see his face in the shadows that fell on him. He had closed his eyes and stood on the rug. His face looked bruised, especially his cheekbones. His eyes remained closed for a while, as he folded his arms around his waist and held on to his elbows. He was mumbling something. Religious, without a doubt. This may not be him, I thought.

Then with his eyes closed, he slowly lifted his arms and held the palms of his hands to his ears. I could hear him mumbling again, and his voice seemed to emerge out of somewhere between his nostrils and his throat. After a few seconds, he bent over and his hands touched his knees. And he sighed in the most reconciled manner. An unforgettable sigh. I had heard it repeatedly, many years ago. This just could be him!

It is said that when you are mesmerized easily, it is probably because you are either a child who has been waiting for a gift that has been denied to you for some time or a poet who has experienced something that no one else has. Or an inexperienced intern in a litigation firm in a city in a country that pretends to be the embodiment of neutrality and has, for the first time, experienced how fabrications and conjectures could be wrapped around facts and made to look innocuously graceful and statutory. Overall, I was stunned that I was seeing him again.

I was neither an innocent, any longer, nor a poet, but definitely a mesmerized lawyer looking for a long-lost childhood friend and mentor. I was pretty sure now that it was him. It is a moment when the world stops on its axis, the wind halts, the sunlight breaks through the vertiginous darkness in a forest, when a branch decides to shoot out, making for an opening at the top. Stillness takes over. One is no longer in absolute control of oneself.

My hands fell to my sides and I could hear myself sighing, as well. I must have exhaled too insolently. The dogs in the alley, on the Strand, who had all gone to sleep, would perk themselves up and howl as if they had heard that familiar exhalation of comfort and resignation. I was unable to control it. My fifty-five-year-old corpus went slack, my knees buckled a bit, my nerves released its hold and I lost my balance. My legs stepped to the side and that he heard. His eyes opened and he looked gently towards me, as I stood in the darkness. I saw him, as well—there was a stream of red still oozing out of a wound on his right temple; his hair, a mix of grey, black and silver, matted, fell over his eyes.

He then dropped to his knees and bowed his head till his forehead touched the rug on the ground.

After he had done this about five times, he stood up and turned around to look at me. A smile emerged. The blood on his temple was still seeping out.

"Shaf?" I asked.

"Binyamin! As salamu alaykum!" He responded.

I hesitated a bit, before I responded, "Waʿalaykumu s-salām!"

We had met again after more than forty years.

"You are coming back with me. That is why I drove," I said.

On that day, March 11, 1985, Mikhail Gorbachev was elected General Secretary of the Soviet Communist Party by the Politburo.

Chapter Two

My father was in and out of the house. A quiet character. He talked gently, whispered into my mother's ears, hugged me and my sister, and then went away. He would be gone for a few weeks, sometimes months, and then he would reappear.

I remember that when I was four or five, his appearances would be auspicious. Like a spiritual happening. He would appear unannounced. As he stepped in through the door, like a leopard looking around, but with a smile, he would take off his beret, dip his head, the door frame being slightly smaller than his height. And then he would move the shabby lace curtain aside and smile in a manner that overwhelmed me, like life had rebounded back! His grace was overwhelming. My body shook, my lips quivered. I stood silly for a few seconds and then I screamed.

"Bo is here! Bo is here!"

How I concocted that word for father, I do not know. But there is a possibility that my mother's cousin who, visited us once in a while, used the word Abba to describe the father and the way she pronounced it, I only heard the second syllable, Ba. It was possible that she did not open her mouth adequately, due to several missing teeth in the front. And I repeated whatever I heard and absorbed in a piercing soprano shriek. Because that is exactly how I felt. And Ba was made into Bo. So, Ba or Abba, Ab, Baba was the universal word for father in Persian, Turkish, Bengali, Hebrew, Hausa, Shona, Swahili, Punjabi, Albanian or Mandarin, amongst others (as I learnt much later in my life). All those who had passed through these mountains, the rivers in the valley below, who built towns and villages along the way, married each other and spoke different languages that often sounded similar, were more or less culturally syncretic. For a thousand years, whether on horseback, foot or armoured carriers, soldiers, conquerors, invaders, priests, imams, rabbis, bridge builders and bridge destroyers—all venerated the father, I had decided. For me, Bo was the word that stood for guide, saint and teacher. I am not sure that my father always felt that he deserved such honours, but irrespective, he stood there as a hero at the threshold.

My mother stood at the far end of the first room, leaning against the dark wood door frame, with an amazingly stunning, but cynical smile. Like a gentle shower after a dank grey day. Grateful tears swelled up in her eyes, when he walked in, but she reined in her enthusiasm, by slowly closing her eyes at my tiresome and worshipful attitude towards my father. She felt an enormous sense of relief. Even though he would stay only for a few weeks. And, when my father left, I saw the back of his head, as he pulled aside the curtain and stepped outside. A thinning hairline, covered by a black beret, faded away. We heard him open the outer door, shut it silently and then he was gone. I stared as the curtain swung back to its normal position my fingers from both hands locked into each other tight, my lips pursed. The oxygen that was already depleted, got sucked out completely.

My mother went back into the next room. She did not like to see him leave. She had very little to do with my father's side of the family. She entered this family, only because my father must have pursued her vigorously and of course he was irresistibly attractive, as well. She knew his qualities, as well as his tendencies. He had capabilities that others in the family did not. They had met in college while attending a polytechnic to the north of us. She was in an institute that was famous worldwide, for physics and magnetism. He was doing his baccalaureate in physiology or biology. From what I had figured out, my mother abandoned her future in magnetism and followed the force field my father generated into what could best be construed as the double life of a doctor and a covert rebel. He transferred from town to town, village to village, country to country—until he surprised us by saying that he was registered in a London College to study medicine. Whether that was a ploy or a career move, was never resolved.

My Mama was agreeable to having a child at that point and so they came back and settled in this valley where my grandfather had considerable leverage as a public official, as a law-and-order kind of guy, and with some concealed political tendencies that became increasingly apparent later to townsfolk. Of course, my parents knew what he was, in reality. Above all this, he was the public prosecutor. My mother once clearly stated what she felt. *When a monkey wears a cassock and advises a judge, then there is bound to be hell in the nation.* Something like that. She made that up, I am sure. Simple, but worth considering, those days. So, Nika was born. My sister, that is—when my parents were in their early twenties.

And, some eight years later, I appeared—possibly unexpectedly, but nevertheless in harmonious consonance with the roar of the first Messerschmitt Bf 109 Es which emerged in the skies over Europe. Soon after, came the screaming and whistling sounds of bombs that came careening down from the clouds. Some months later, I heard the terrifying sounds of 500KG bombs landing some distance away beyond the outskirts of our town, followed by the thundering air displacements that rushed through the whole house. But nothing landed on our town, near the stone bridge over the canal or the Strand around it. We cowered in a pantry that had been constructed by my Bo a few steps below the actual kitchen. It was designed for four people to stay put. Unfortunately it was such a mess that to get in there we stepped over sacks of salt, flour and more flour. For sure, when the all-clear sirens wailed, we would come out looking pretty powdered up.

***

Certain Friday evenings after dinner, Bo gave my sister some history lessons. If he was around. I listened in. My mother sat down in the corner on a dark green leather chair, lit a eucalyptus-scented candle and read Russian novels. Occasionally she would turn her head and smile at the lessons that were ongoing. I sat on a small stool, listening or spinning a top.

"Just a few years before you were born, the Ottoman Empire was finally falling apart. Coming to its end. From February 1915 to January 1916, the Entente—that is Russia, France and Britain—thought it would be nice to give a fine drubbing to the Ottomans while they were on their last legs. On the British side was an arrogant, plump, bulldog of a personality named . . . what? Any guesses?"

And he looked at Nika. My Mama smiled, while her eyes remained on Turgenev.

"Who? I don't know!" Nika said, with a curious smile.

"Of course, you won't. And it won't be taught either, in history classes."

My mother turned around at the way my father controlled his audience.

"The name of that rotund character, known for his cliches, was a certain Winston Churchill. Head of the Admiralty of Britain. Remember that name. It will come up frequently from now on. And you will also hear a little bit about the Battle of Gallipoli and the Battle of the Dardanelles."

"Yes, we did, but not much. It's quite recent though." Nika commented and I listened with undivided attention. In my head, I took notes.

"Indeed! The Entente made a covert move to finish off the Turks! But they were in for a surprise. In the history books you won't hear about who got the drubbing."

"Who got the drubbing?" Nika did not seem seriously interested. She was teasing my Bo.

"Well! A combined land and sea invasion was planned. It highly underestimated the capacity of the Turks to defend the seaways around them. And their capital Constantinople. For years to come, you will see that this area—the Black Sea coast, the sea of Marmara, the Dardanelles would come to be known as a key area of contention. And why this area, you may ask."

"And why this area, I ask!" Nika was being very annoying.

"It is because it is a narrow strait with lots of ports. And because access to the Black Sea is access to Russia! Access to the Suez is reserved for the British Empire only! Control of these two areas will forever be like a chess game. Between the East and the West! It's that fat man, Churchill, the Lord of the Admiralty, who was the one who got his pudgy face drubbed in oil and tar. And who did it?"

"Ataturk?" Nika knew that.

"That's right! Kemal Pasha Ataturk! He changed everything. A gaunt and suave man. He knew things had to change. But he was also ready to confront!" It seemed like my Bo had a thing for him.

"And he was not a fat, pudgy guy! Right?" Nika piped in. There were some giggles in the room. My mother turned away from her book again and smiled. Turgenev was not that exciting, anyway. It was getting a bit chilly outside. My Mama came and put a shawl on Nika. I was already wearing a warm sweater. My Bo was somehow distracted and looking away. Imagining his next trip.

"He declared the end of the Ottoman Empire and formed Turkey, changed its laws, decreed equal power to women and did a lot of things to unify the country. And that is about the time when you were born." He pointed at me. Saying that, he got up and went into the bedroom.

***

In the years to come, as I became a lawyer, I grasped fully that the objectives of *nations, governments, and the citizens* did not always converge. They were three separate entities. It did not matter how much one wanted justice and fairness inside one's own country; what mattered was that nations or countries, little and big kingdoms, had to align themselves with nearby or even distant military and economic powers to protect themselves. Justice was merely an afterthought, a side effect.

The royalist enclaves, puny at times but mostly incestuous in how they held on to land and property by intermarrying, were fixated about blood lines and religious phobias. Declarations of ethnic differences would be emphasized and insulting each other with words and weapons would result in redefining maps and boundaries. But in the end, the sextant that was used would gage who would control the seaways, ports and trade routes. That was the big picture. And the peasants squabbled for land and liberty, till they dropped dead on their hoes and on the ramparts outside the castle walls.

In our country, there was a small section for whom religious and ethnic differences mattered. Bo was annoyed with them. They warmed up to the ideas of Adolph and his chum Benito.

But the majority in our country were only small players in a much larger canvas. The Tower tilted above them perilously. My father, in one of his Friday lectures, pointed out that the *Peasant Wedding* was a greater work than the *Tower of Babel* and so the latter had no place in our dining room. The former was hung up, above the dinner wagon, at somewhat of a careless tilt. And as I looked closely at all the faces, I saw no desperation, no anger, no frustration. Just a gathering where sharing, conversing and catching up on each other's lives was important. Because the next morning, with hoes on their shoulders, they had to head for the fields or to their battle stations.

The walls of our sitting room, which was like the second room in our cottage (out of a total of five including a corner for a kitchen), was stuccoed carelessly and so the fines from the nearby bauxite factory settled along the raised edges of each contour on the wall and left a dark residue. My mother cooked and fried a type of battered chicken, which she bashed with a dough roller with such viciousness that the supporting beams for both of the two adjoining rooms shook, never mind the table on which she carried out the assault until the chicken gave up, its breasts cracked open. My mother was whipping up several chicken eggs next, with a similarly volatile energy level.

"Mama, are you angry?"

She would break out of her maniacal spell, put everything down and pick me up with a glorious smile. The fumes from the frying which spiralled up and hung concentrated at an adult shoulder level, were then ingested by me with a suffocating intensity as my mother carried me around the house. I did not complain.

"Could I be mad at you, Ben? Do you really think I could? Sometimes I should, though, what do you say?"

Deep warmth on the bosom of my Mama made me squirm and so did the open-ended question at the end. Which made me think of possibilities where I could totally wreck her day, if I wanted to. As she walked me around the house, to calm down my fears about her furious attack on the chicken breasts, I took the opportunity to run my fingers along the walls. The oily fumes which caked and glued the dust in the air into the rounded contours of the stucco could not be removed unless you washed it with a scrubber. That device was a natural sponge fibre brush that she kept hanging from the kitchen windowsill, and that cleaning would happen perhaps once in two years, maybe, when Bo would be around for more than three weeks. Until then the walls remained sticky. My mother walked around the house with me in her arms, chatting me up about how farm animals sounded all together, like when they debated important issues in the town.

"The chickens say, 'Hey! We need more corn around here. Where's the corn now? Where's the mayor? Is anybody holding it back? What's the matter with these pig heads? Down with the pigs! Do we not count?'"

"The pigs would then stir out of the kaka they were sleeping in and grunt, 'Go somewhere else, dung brains. Find your own corn. You don't belong here. Go back to where you came from.'"

I remember that pig and chicken fable, vividly. And my Mama made horrendous sounds with her nose and throat, mimicking the pigs who apparently ruled the plains and the chickens who were treated like serfs. But as my Mama explained, the chickens and the pigs were not seeing the light of day! They ought to find common ground, because it was the bigger animals that lived deep in the forests like cheetahs, leopards and hyenas that could swoop down from the dark forests further up in the mountains, grab the chickens or simply bite off the faces of the biggest pigs and take them back into the forest. The chickens and the pigs had to strike a deal, she said.

Sometimes we stared out of the window at the gentle hills that rolled up into large mountains. And beyond, we could see the river glisten through the greenery. She would peel oranges, sitting at the table alone, soaking them in brandy that my father had brought back from Germany and readying them for a pie. And she would stare out again with that livid look, building up slowly.

My sister would swoop down from a back room and take two orange segments straight from the bowl they were soaking in, while it was still warm, and prance away with a totally mischievous smile. She lived in the back room. Nika went to a college run by nuns, somewhere up in the hills. And she went by a bus service, whose route through the front of our house was arranged by some mysterious patron we would need to be indebted to. My grandfather knew what was good for us.

A prosecutor at the local courts, my grandfather lived in another section of the family complex, which was entirely enclosed by walls. The walls were painted in a dusty, pale-yellow pigment, with brickwork exposed here and there. Along the top of the walls there were slate tiles sloping outward. The tiles and the compound wall had been painted a few years ago, and some sort of a tapestry done on one of the walls by a local farmer's brother, an artist, was still discernible. It was like a declaration of his fealty to my grandfather. Obvious, ugly and even mysterious. But, perhaps mischievous too. There would be a baronic figure sitting on a throne with two accomplices, whispering to each other, behind him. Like pusillanimous yea-sayers. And then there were some harp-like instruments, mandolins, little trinkets like stars, the moon, a happy sun face, painted in a collage in the sky, a bridge in the distance and more stars and a cross, like bibelots drawn here and there, to hang up like ornaments in the make over world the artist had been commissioned to erect. And next to these little harps, there was a man bowing down, like a serf.

All this had been painted over, but I knew the tapestry by heart. It could not be erased even if you put a generation of painters to whitewash that wall. It was still visible to my eyes, as though the paint-over was also done purposefully and imperfectly. As if to reveal to a passerby that loyalties change, and history lies beneath layers. That behind each image, there could be a tapestry concealed, from a previously victorious raider and occupier. That some colours ran so deep and dark that a pale covering would not suffice. Murals in museums, in mosques, churches and synagogues often got easily plastered over. Until lack of moisture or acid in the air would make that plaster start to get too brittle, powdery and trickle down on worshippers, who would look up in amazement, as images from another era, another ruler's religious and doctrinal beliefs, would start to appear.

Our family complex was designed to look like some sort of a local baron's hacienda or castle complex. It was the only one in the village, with a wrought iron gate and walls all around it. There was a garden right in the middle, surrounded by a walkway, which had once been a pebbled path. Circular, it took you right up to my grandfather's round-domed Byzantine house. When my grandfather stepped out of his building and stood between four pillars on the porch and put his thumbs into the sides of his waist coat pockets and looked out, the world around him stood tentative, immobilized. I noticed him from the small window in our bathroom. His well-waxed moustache moved a twitch and then settled down. He cleaned his teeth after breakfast by rolling his tongue around in his mouth. He did not realize that I was watching him. He never came into our five rooms. But we did go and meet him once in a while.

He would look up in the skies, as the droning sound from warplanes far away seemed to make him put his chest out. Then a two-horse phaeton arrived to pick him up. A servant or some kind of a helper allocated by the district jumped out, carried his briefcase—black and shiny crocodile leather with brass buckles and locks—and opened the door for him. And he was gone. Not to be back till five in the evening. The same Serf-like creature who had carried his briefcase out in the morning would jump out with it and would deposit it at the doorstep, where a handsome looking maid and cook, stood waiting and she would carry it in.

The Serf. I have remembered the Serf forever.

As I grew up, I began to have a better understanding of my grandfather's stature in the village and in the district where our town was located. He had a compelling reputation as a prosecutor, no mercy in his veins. An imposing and infernally angry creature from Hades, with a self-proclaimed notion of command and control of whatever he purveyed. The town was about fifteen minutes away by horse cart or bicycle from the village we lived in. Often, he raised his voice in public meetings, and everyone would turn around and go into a silent mode. As a public prosecutor, and therefore a senior government administrator, he was fiercely independent and often berated those who were senior to him in the district administration. He was pungent in his condemnation of a local councillor in our municipality, who had had the gall to call for monthly dinners amongst councillors and citizens from various ethnic and religious backgrounds. That should have been a significant signal for me.

It took me a while to realize that an assortment of opinions, proclamations and reactions of a personality do not predict the ultimate inclinations of the person, early enough. He was into cleanliness, hygiene and spotlessness and one reason he did not come into our house was because my mother had no inclination for following the norms of a family she was not born into and had limited respect for order and cleanliness. Making bread, getting the food on the table, taking me to school and being extraordinarily comforting and warm to me and my sister was as far a distance she was prepared to travel. At some point she chose not to help me any longer with Geometry, Algebra or for that matter language studies and History as she decided to deploy a private tutor. Now that was a bit later.

We were not poor at all. My mother inherited some wealth from her side of the family. My father seemed to have no problem either. But a kind of disinheritance loomed large in my horizon.

***

This town was named Sabzic more than five hundred years ago by a colourful raider named Prince Diedar, a pleasant man on horseback from the mountains beyond, probably from another valley all together, or perhaps from the other side of the world. He was an independent stallion rider and raider, not assigned by any Sultan or Prince or any caliphate, kingdom or empire. As far as raiders go, it was said that he was of a peculiar pedigree. Got easily bored and took counselling from various religious leaders on food, soil, astronomy and medicine. At some point, due to a chance encounter with a Mongol nomad tribe near the Black Sea, he walked into a tent where he came under the influence of a Buddhist monk. Whereupon, he became a stringent vegetarian and discouraged animal slaughter. In a time like that, I would have thought that devouring animals would keep the body warm.

When he reached this part of the world, he settled down in no time, because he loved the clear waters that rippled through the valley and the lush green fields, where small farmers grew what they needed and nothing more. He named the town Sabzic, which was derived from the Persian word for greenery and herbs. The trees on the banks, stood their ground, clawing the earth as the water rushed down in spring from the mountains. He lined the river banks with trees with extraordinary precision. About fifty feet apart and all following the curves in the river. And the river had apparently never changed course since, but he had managed to tame it enough to divert a part of it into a canal. An extraordinary way, indeed, to prevent erosion—making a bypass into the lower edge of the valley and thereby creating a placid setting for a town by the edge of the canal. The canal then flowed back into the river, downstream. It created a picturesque island, with the town innately serene with pale yellow houses, intensely green shrubbery and an endless stream of visitors and traders, who prized the town of Sabzic for its unique placement at the bottom of the mountains and being an enclave of melting cultures. Because of his Buddhist inclinations, I was also told that there was some throat singing in the mosques at times. Sabzic brought food and music from the surrounding countries and an ambience that produced a state of happiness. A sense of *spellbound brotherhood* prevailed. That is the expression my father used, with a smirk.

Prince Diedar listened to the music of the valley and got so absorbed in the local songs and musical instruments, and the food that was cooked here, that he parked all his war horses in a large stable he had built, and had the farmers use them for tilling the soil. Almost like a contract arrangement. He sat impassively on a large woolen carpet, listening to the music played by locals. I also found out that a large number of families in our town, also chose to be vegetarian. We were not.

In conversations with my mother, I came to know that Prince Diedar was a devout Muslim, but an independent one. He called conclaves of priests, imams and rabbis to discuss health issues, drainage, soil erosion and the nutrition provided by various vegetables that grew in the valley. He discussed astronomy and mathematics and most of all he went into a silent trance listening to the music of this valley.

According to my father—and I suspect he had extrapolated all this from the information tableaus about Diedar in our local town library and, as well, injected his own fabulous storytelling skills—Diedar had managed to conflate the music of our valley with that of the music he had listened to as a child in the mountains to the north where he had come from. His conviction, according to my mother, was that his people must have also come to this valley, several centuries ago. He found meaning in the correspondence in the names of towns, the vegetables grown here, the names of musical instruments and popular expressions.

My father in his droll style explained to me that if he had been around at that time, he would have explained to Diedar that there were only four or five root languages thousands of years ago. I learnt that all the tribes and nations that grew out of this range of mountains and valleys melded into each other and could not escape the influence of Indo-European, Germanic, Slavic, and Romance languages. Language and words came long before churches and mosques or priests and pulpits. The words may not sound alike, but they used an overabundance of common words. And, based on the sustained stay of invaders and their religions, the names of towns would change a bit here and there, but sometimes they also got totally obliterated, like the tapestries that had faded away in the walls of our complex.

My grandfather did not like this conviviality. This pleasantness, warmth and hospitality was not to his liking. He tweaked his moustache in disgust.

My father was away in the UK and I was about nine years old when a fellow by the name of Neville Chamberlain

36

declared war on Germany on September 3, 1939. Two days earlier, an erratic, vain, evil and comical German fellow named Adolph, had marched into Poland.

It is at this time, when planes emerged in diamond formations from inside grim clouds and flew closer and closer to our pastel-pale town. With perfect timing my grandfather sneaked in a motion in the town council to change the name of the village from Sabzic to Goshtlow. It was not exactly a Christian name, but according to him, this new name would ward off some annoying religious and vegetarian propensities.

During these times, I would hear an elderly Romani man— perhaps a hawker—walk by our house and keep repeating in a monotonous voice, the phrase *from dusk to dawn, from dusk to dawn* over and over again.

Chapter Three

Often when I stepped out of our house onto the front steps, I would tug at the suspenders holding up my shorts. They were designed to look like dangling wine barrels rather than shorts. If it were not for the sun's rays that made me squint my six-year-old eyes, I would take a furtive glance to the right, to see if my grandfather was on his front porch, looking out. My grandfather would notice from a distance and grin. It was like a smirk—*"boy, pull up your pants!"* If our eyes met, I would wave to him and he would simply nod his head while I squinted and tugged, alternately. At times I was compelled to walk the long, tortuous path to his porch and be ensnared into a conversation. He would be waiting for his ride or simply sitting on the porch on an ornate, gold-painted, upholstered chair with silk embroidery, delivered to him by a Venetian businessman who had brought in "contraband" without the necessary paperwork. Years later, I would be nodding to myself, not surprised, as to how a public prosecutor could lessen the charges, when it seemed his very job required him to pile them on. My sister Nika, significantly shrewder, knew him well and would not even look at the preposterously throned individual to the right of her. She ambled along to the front gate with a swirl of her head and waited outside for her bus to come along, outside the line of vision of *the Baron*. On non-college days, she would be out for a walk or a bus ride somewhere. She was much older than I. I really did not know where she went, but she always came back with her cheeks crimson, and the scarlet red scarf around her neck added to the inscrutability. Even on a warm day. Being naughty is a concept I understood then as a challenge towards parental restrictions, impositions, etc. I came to realize later that it was an impatience about the display of reserve expected of girls of her age and, even later on, it dawned on me that it was an assertion of a growing independence, away from the family, on her part. My parents were not very restrictive, but Nika did things I marvelled at doing. Outstanding stuff. Like when she found the toilet was occupied by my Bo, she would simply go out, walk over to behind my grandfather's little Roman-pillared back porch, lift up her skirt, pull down her knickers and flood the cemented patio. Then she would skip back laughing, because she knew I would have seen her doing it.

My mother, despite her disgust and distaste for the attitudes and leanings of my grandfather, had instructed me to dip my head in acknowledgement of his presence under the portico. From a distance. And then I was free to go and play in the yard that was in front of our house. Sometimes, I could not avoid going and talking to my grandfather. Nika? She never even thought he existed. A distinct attitude set-up early on. Like the glochids on a cactus despite the attractive blooms, she provided advance warning.

His first question to me was always—"What did you eat for breakfast, today?"

39

"Pie, sausages and milk." I would say in a distracted fashion, because it was a partial lie. I had no milk. I disliked milk. He would check regularly if I was having milk. But I was crazy about the corn-flour pies my mother made in the oven. They were flaky, crispy, dripping in butter and salted with an exuberance that I later realized was because my mother found great joy in sprinkling the sodium chloride from a foot above the pan in smooth dance moves, as would a sorceress, without an audience.

Then my grandfather would carry on, in his grim voice—"Is your Bo back? Where is he, do you know?"

"England." I would say. "Studying to be a doctor."

"Really? Is he serious this time? No more chemistry and biology then, I suppose. Anatomy, it is!"

I would not even bother to think that out. All I saw of my Bo was that he came and went, smiled and held me close, before he left and then he hugged Nika and kissed my mother and disappeared. If he was studying medicine, he should have been smelling better. His long winter jacket often smelled like he had been milking cows in a barn where other animals also congregated, either to be milked or slaughtered. The pork tenderloin my mother bought from an adjoining piggery was not that smelly. It came all tied up and smelly, but when she sizzled them in a frying pan, with more than a handful of garlic buds, browned them all over with herbs and butter, they were crisp on the outside and buttery on the inside. It is what my Bo loved the most. The mystery man was Bo and Mama was the medicine woman! And he had it with chunks of bread, which he ripped from the loaf, much to her annoyance. Especially since she had put a bread knife in front of his eyes. But she would not say anything. Every time, he came back from wherever he went,

40

she was simply too happy to see him, smell and all, and did not want to pester him. She would watch him from the other side of the kitchen table, sipping her coffee from an outsized enamel mug he had brought back for her from one of his previous trips. The smile on her face was like that of some Italian actress on a poster that hung in their bedroom. Sweet, happy and sad, at the same time. Like, memories were slipping away and the sadness would brim over soon, from somewhere deep inside. I did not miss any emotions but I never understood what all their words meant. It sailed over my head, but the looks and the exchanges got branded into my memory banks. My parents' space was so welcoming compared to my grandfather's aura of vitriol, vinegar and rancour sprayed into the space around him.

"So, how's college? Are the anatomy sessions challenging?" And she winked, and I did not miss that. It was her way of forcing him out of his shy demeanour.

After some hesitation, my Bo looked around to see if I was watching them and a curt smile appeared on his lips as he did not miss a chance to tease her back.

"And the magnetic fields around you? How are they? Maxwells? Coulombs? Do you feel it? We shall find out soon! Hein?"

A mouthful of the bread and he looked up at her.

My father's retort would be hopelessly awkward. All this did not escape me. It seemed like they spoke in code, but deep inside there was a mischievous and intelligent wavelength their love was transmitted in, in front of their Algebra-challenged son.

My mother accompanied me to school and we chatted non-stop all the way. I was interested in History, languages and how things were managed in cities and towns. And I had a fascination for rocks. Yes, rocks! I picked up small pieces randomly, if I found them of interest, and put them in my satchel. But it was the boulder-like pieces that I found more interesting. I stopped to examine them. I knew my mother followed all my actions, closely.

I found in rocks the signatures of dwellers and citizens from different times who may have passed through the valley. I do not mean the hieroglyphics, but just the way rocks were positioned as road markers, even at the bus stops. And how more and more of them were shaped like square blocks that reflected the way cutting tools had been developed by artisans and tool makers. Rocks did not tumble down and cause avalanches if they had a square and flat base. Smartly positioned rocks, one on top of the other and spaced properly, would allow towers and bridges to stand firm for centuries. That was intriguing for me. While in high school—I had just started to learn about Geometry and a little bit of Algebra—I was just as interested in the physics of stability as in the advances made by society in being able to cut rocks in geometric shapes, so that they would attest to the way people chose to live together or away from each other. Mark territory, roads, symbols, borders and brain impulses that pulsed along and changed the way people lived in communities.

The rocks had to be cut in quarries, then hauled off in carts or trucks. Then they would be dumped in a field somewhere near the city. Contractors would buy the rocks and use them for landscaping, road designations, building the bases and towers for stone bridges, building cellars and dividing roads as well. This stuff registered in a cumbersome way. My Mama pointed out something unique.

"The rocks have to be heavy enough, so that bandits do not carry them away at night. Only special trucks could carry them."

"But that is only now. What happened at the time of Diedar?" I asked.

"I guess the rocks were smaller and horse carts could carry them."

I was very proud of my observations. I remember that some of the huge concrete blocks had fading Arabic writing carved onto them. In many of them the writing had been ground out.

The municipality bought the rocks, shaped them for road dividers and, as well, broke them up and put them in as cobblestones, as they did for a couple of centuries. The municipality also built the Strand around the canal. That required a significant amount of collaboration. The town administration had to acquire land around the canals, flatten the area around it, chop down some of the trees that Prince Diedar had put up some centuries ago. Eventually by the 1750s—Dukes, Vazirs, Barons, Counts, Sultans and the occasional raiders and occupiers had built wrought-iron railings around the canal, where townsfolk could walk around.

I noticed how the big bolts would be inserted into the rocks to hold up the railings. Rust had started to chew up the bolts and nuts, which made the holes oblong and the rocks would slip out of symmetry along the sides of the canal. The symmetricity and congruency, the fit, along the sides of the canal were dissipating. Parts of Sabzic were desolate, in disrepair and losing its orderliness. And that is when the bombs started whistling down and falling somewhere in the mountains beyond.

I never did well in Arithmetic, never mind Geometry and Algebra much later. By the time I was nine or ten, my mother had been recommended by the headmaster to avail the services of a private tutor, because I was not doing my homework. My mother agreed, as they knew that my sister was not particularly strong in the Sciences either. Nevertheless, Nika in her flowing black skirt, with an embroidered blue band running all along the edge, was always there when Shaf came to the house, twice a week, to supervise my Algebra homework on equations. It was my father who had engaged this very handsome, quiet, tall man to make me understand the sequence of quadratics and the features of isosceles within isosceles.

He came from a town across the canal, where he taught Physics to college students. What I learnt from him was beyond the material that the schoolteacher offered up to me. He gave me life lessons. The schoolteacher gave me lifeless homework.

***

"There is an issue of fit here, a size-to-size mating of parts that make the whole. The individual parts must stay in shape, otherwise the overall fit gets undermined. Rectilinearity is lost. Now the question is how do you keep the fit, huh? Young fella?"

Shaf would walk around the room, while I did my homework on triangles. He would not always be sitting under the lamp. In a world of his own, mumbling often to himself. He himself told me that he did not like to be a monitor in school. He said once he walked out of the classroom while lecturing and did not realize that he was outside till it was time to present his conclusion on the subject.

"Did the students wait for you?"

"Yes, I think they did."

"It is intimidating and unnerving for the student, or the young child like you, to be constantly lectured. Is it not?" And when he said child, it was emphatic. I felt some meanness there. Like he had broken out of some inner thoughts and distanced himself from me. He was here only because of my Bo, whom he respected greatly. He approached my homework attempts like it was not only Algebra, but also the psychology of letting young children like me not be pushed towards a life of doing repetitive work, which they did not enjoy. I agreed. And I actively diverted him into discussion topics that were remotely related to homework. He obliged easily. This attracted me to him, considerably, because it brought my interaction with him to a different level. As an example, he started talking about subjects that were not in the homework or even the course books. Like the concept of the astronomical unit, the traverse of Venus across the Sun and stuff like infinity, as an example. But of that later.

His eyes—soft, tender and unpredictable—were also looking over my shoulders and scanning the table with the responsibility my parents had accorded him. He would, from a distance, note that I was not following the rules of solving for what was inside the brackets, before doing anything else, and would approach me quickly, before I would cause further damage in balancing equations—you know the stuff about LHS=RHS. He would come at me with a gentle smile and stop my inattentive efforts, by pointing to the rules that said, brackets come first.

BODMAS!

And there were occasions, we would walk down the side of the canal, despite the fact that I was only ten years old.

My Mama had no problems with that. A different kind of education would ensue.

In various detours, we would discuss the rectilinearity of rock placements along the sides of the canal for over three hundred years and many topics were taken up, including and up to this period of the beginning of the Second World War. For example, the borders of countries that were redrawn randomly. The towns and cities that fell to armies who believed in the need for strong leaders or a one-country-one-leader type rule, or those who opposed such authoritarianism and spoke of alliances of their own. My mother, my father and my tutor agreed with each other so overwhelmingly that I was at a loss as to how there could be any opposing views to theirs. I realized later that they were like a tightly knit group of intractable rebels, perhaps too well informed than the general population. That could be a problem.

And on the opposite side, stood my grandfather under the porch, with his thumbs inside his vest pocket, moustache waxed and twirled, committed to law and order and discipline. And I also noticed that there were huge cobwebs that grew under the ceiling in the corner of his porch. There were large black spiders waiting to drop down daringly on an insipid day when there were no winds. I wished they did. That could be a problem also.

"When Kings and Queens reached a low point in their rule, because they never really had a worldwide presence, and their national currency had little impact on trade, they took to aligning themselves with nearby Dukes or Sultans to protect their enclaves. Physical protection, that is. It is the kind of kingdom or state, where the thickness of walls and the diameters of the cannons were a deciding factor."

46

I heard what Shaf had to say, but did not absorb all this entirely till much later. Eventually the people fell into the orbit of one Axis or the other. While the Royalty opted for an alignment, the rest of the nation did not find it particularly appealing. Some military officers rebelled, staged a coup and that is when all hell descended upon the valley. Something like that. It was a combination of my conclusions with the gentle persuasion of my mentor and teacher, Shaf. From the technology of shaping rocks and defining boundaries to the strewing of bodies in trenches, it was a different kind of mathematics that he prodded me on to.

On April 6, 1941, the bombs started falling: in the hills around us with increased intensity; in airports on the other side of the country; and the ground shook in a steady and continuous rumble all through the day and the night. Our Kingdom was invaded from all sides.

For ten days, the nation's capital was bombed. While surrender was an unacceptable option, it did happen and my grandfather actually applauded. He looked up in the sky and almost wanted to be blessed by falling bombs. That is the day I got everything clear as to where he stood and my tuition giver was deeply concerned, not only because of my grandfather's leanings, but also for his own safety. I did not understand exactly why he kept coming in to oversee my tuition. When my mother went to pay him his fees, he even declined some of it. Such details are clear to me. He took some money but not all. And on one of those days, while I put on a grand show of following the rules of BODMAS, Nika—in a flowing black skirt with a blue embroidered trim—careened past us by swinging the curtain aside and actually putting her hand on Shaf's shoulder. Then she left by the front door, smiling but worried. I was quite amused and felt mischievous, but looked down at plus and minus signs and various types of brackets while a wayward fleeting fragrance drifted away. And the earth trembled a bit as Nika skipped away and Shaf turned around to look at her.

The big capital city, to the north of us, was bombed by the Luftwaffe. It was ten days of unabated, ground-trembling carpet bombing. Our King and his entourage surrendered unconditionally. Our national army, poorly equipped and stretched, had to take on many armies and suddenly there were many borders. The slaughter was complete.

"Look at the cowardice of our people in not being man enough. We deserve it," said my grandfather, teasing away at his coiled moustache.

The Germans were seen as liberators of our people. In this complex situation, some ethnic groups turned to any movement that was intrinsically against overall national unity. This left two options for the people who wanted to resist: first were the royalists; and then there were the partisans, who were communists in essence. At least two of the ethnic groups would not have anything to do with the overbearing domination by the larger segment of the population. They also refused to support the monarchy.

It seemed like almost all the countries that were around us, chose to align with the Germans and walked in and took over whatever chunks of land they could. Sabzic, minimally touched by direct bombing, became, very soon, a fertile space for the flowering of my grandfather's political beliefs.

On May 27, 1941, the British navy sank the newly launched German battleship, the Bismarck, in the Atlantic, off the coast of France. My grandfather was sulking that afternoon.

Chapter Four

As the bombs reportedly came gliding down in the mountains to the north of us, like fish entrails, as described by Nika, and were accompanied by the distant sounds of machine guns both from the sky and the ground, my history lessons became more important than the rules of solving equations.

My mother looked up into the night sky and I knew she was thinking about Bo, who had not been back for over a month. Shaf would come to the house twice a week. He rode a bicycle and parked under a tree outside the pale-yellow wall. The plaster on the wall kept trickling down to reveal murals that had been made by vassals to gratify the owner of the property. He walked in quietly, as my grandfather watched him closely from the throne on his porch. My sister ran in and out of the room where I got my history lessons, as if she had something to say. I noticed her demure smile as she went about this fictitious activity.

As far as history lessons go, Shaf had the peculiar habit of interrogating himself as he went about presenting the topic that he had to cover. He made a statement and then challenged it. I realized years later in college that there were very few lecturers like him. This methodology of teaching, of questioning themselves and their beliefs in front of students, was a good way to instigate a subtext to everything that was official and in the textbook, without sabotaging the text as such. Most lecturers and professors would go about covering the topic, exactly as in the book.

"It went on for five hundred years. Between Christians and Muslims, the see-saw battles for controlling territories resulted in Kings, Dukes and Vazirs—Orthodox, Catholic, Byzantine, Ottoman, Turks, Greeks, Mongols, Genoese, Venetians and others—building armies and navies and knocking the hell out of each other on land and sea. But what do you think they were really after?" he asked himself. "What were they looking for? Horses? Food that they did not grow? Weapons and equipment?"

He looked at the wall or looked through the window as he covered these topics.

"What about gold, copper?" I had said. He stared at me, as if I would help him further with the answer.

The week before, he had fallen off his bike. He had grazed his knee on one of the big rocks stationed along the sides of the canal. There was some bleeding. It showed through his white pants. I pointed it out and he informed me about the incident.

"It's nothing," he said.

Nika appeared from nowhere and started to tend to it. My mother raised one eyebrow and had a smile that slid out from the side of her mouth. I put my chin down on the table as Nika put undue amounts of gauze on the wound and bandaged it up. Shaf looked a bit embarrassed.

"Were they really trying to convert each other? Did they really see themselves as armies of Christ or of the Prophet Mohammed?" he continued. And then he replied to himself.

"Maybe they were looking for security, Ben. Natural boundaries, seas and mountains. The impenetrable wall around Constantinople! The narrow passage around the Golden Horn. The cast iron chain in the sea. What do you think?" What was I to comment on? I had not even given any thought to these things. I tilted my head to the side, shrugged my shoulders, pursed my lips.

"Were Christians looking to convert? Or were they conquering for food and resources? And what were the Ottomans looking at, beyond the hilltops? Were they pursuing the prophecies of the Prophet Mohammed?" His mood shifted.

"And what has always puzzled me is that instead of building physical obstacles, why were they not building observation towers? What do you think?"

"Or balloons?" I said with some enthusiasm.

"Until the seventeenth century, you never really knew who was approaching your borders, till they arrived on the hilltops. The French made use of balloons, but only in the eighteenth century."

His descriptions were vivid. I was tantalized by the idea of balloons.

"But once you conquered, it was like opium drifting through your brains. Afyon! Afyon!"

He said that like he was on stage, like a magician with his eyes sparkling. This was not in the textbook. He walked around the room and I followed his every step, without looking at his face. Such was his charisma, like electricity, when he was in this transported mood! *Afyon!* he said.

"Did the Ottomans win because they had better military weapons?" I asked timidly. He was surprised by this intervention. But it got him going.

"The technology of the Ottomans was far superior to anybody else's at the time. They had dragged their ships over lard-filled land passages through forests that they had cut down and surprised the Byzantine navy from the flanks."

"But that is not technology, that is a crazy and costly battle trick!" I spoke with some confidence.

He whipped around and stared at me. I had caught him by surprise by that retort. He smiled and nodded his head. I knew I had grabbed his attention and perhaps even disrupted his performance. He stopped in his tracks and his smile was quite friendly. I knew from then on we were going to be friends. He walked around and collected his thoughts. We had created chemistry.

"Ben, you raise several complicated questions here."

We suspended our exchange, there, that day.

As a law student much later, I realized that the Ottoman Empire, despite their mission of being the messengers of Allah, had other ideas. In the long run it was best that ordinary people—be they field commanders, *janissaries* and *sipahis*, bridge builders, stone masons, road builders, house builders, farmers and peasants—would all want to come home, make families and settle down in peace. Then they would get to know each other, so that between campaigns, whether they were under siege or conquering, there would be domestic tranquility. People would live as a community, conversing with each other, eating together. Discussing daily issues. Talking in each other's languages. They were laying down the rules for community and nationhood.

Meanwhile, it was Paul, the Saint, who in the first century AD preached in all the provinces in the areas populated by the Greeks and laid down the advent for Christianity.

Made sense to me. Jesus had been martyred and his revolutionary gospel had to be spread—of course with some necessary mystification. And there were a lot of takers. However, did Paul know anything about building communities or nations? It was Emperor Constantine XI, however, who bore the brunt of the collapse and oversaw the sunset over the Eastern Roman or Byzantine Empire.

***

My Bo came back and felt he must intervene in these history lessons.

"The 21-year-old Mehmet II," he said, "settled everything in 1453 in favour of the Ottomans.

"In a three-month siege of the walled city of Constantinople, they broke through the impenetrable walls with Hungarian made twenty-metre-long cannons."

Shaf added on, like he was my father's assistant, "The Byzantine Empire, after 1300, got outdone by the military and diplomatic expertise of the Ottomans. Be it Asia Minor or the entire region where our country is located, the Ottomans built up defensive placements and in fact they did Western Europe a great favour by fighting off all the invaders from further East."

In my ears, I heard big drums, clashing symbols and thundering herds of stallions with armoured warriors astride. They pounded through my grass fields, my mountain tops, my placid valleys and waded through my erratic rivers. They excited me but they also distracted me, immensely. I also learnt over the years that war was not about killing and occupying, who won and who lost—but what ideas triumphed and which ideas wilted and floated away.

"That is right!" Bo said. "Western kingdoms were saved. You name it, 'barbarian' tribes, Venetians, Magyars, other Turkmen made many passes, but the Ottomans laid waste to all and consolidated their rule. Muslims did Christians a great favour! You keep to your piece of the *sirnica*, we keep to ours. Peace be with you! We are building nations here!"

"But that is not in the course material!" I said catching on to where he was headed.

"Of course not!" Bo said and walked over to see what my Mama was up to. He came back a little later with a mug of coffee and continued.

"The Venetians controlled all the trade routes and the prosperity in the fourteenth century got wiped out. Buonaparte, the short one, came by and clipped the wings of the remaining Venetian holdouts in our western flank. The Ottomans ruled supreme, and Western Europe had a field day to rule and conquer in the name of Catholics and the Orthodox. You see what is missing at this point?"

I was not sure, so I did not comment. Shaf continued.

"Well! Napoleon, the short one that is, who could not even speak French well, became Emperor of France, went everywhere from Prussia and Russia to Austria and even Spain. The Ottomans ruled from the fourteenth century to our century, but east of Bonaparte's empire. The French did not try to go to Asia Minor, at that point in time. It was kind of like, leave us alone and we will leave you alone."

Much of our country was under Ottoman rule throughout the Early Modern period. What I learnt eventually, was that it was an ethnically, linguistically and religiously diverse Empire and not merely under Islamic rule.

***

In the early afternoon of July 1, 1939, I was going over the material that Bo and Shaf had thrown at me and I kept writing notes, because all this was not in the history books we were using. There was a knock on the door.

 We rarely had anybody knock on our door because of the walled-in compound and the gate remaining closed. I walked over and opened it, slowly. The maid who looked after my grandfather was standing outside. I had never seen her closely before. She wore a long skirt and a loose blouse and spoke very well. She was elegant and had a long coat, which she wore over her blouse and skirt. I looked at her closely and realized she had rather swarthy, burnt skin. I had never seen her closely. She had a bowl with a lid covering it in her hands. It was hot, from the way she was holding the bowl. She asked if my mother was around and she looked back at the gate in the wall. She seemed a bit jittery. I left the door open and went to call my Mama.

My mother welcomed her and brought her in. She was not very keen to come in. She had made a stew for us. The smell wafted in and spread all over our house. But my Mama insisted and they sat down and chatted at the dinner table. I went to my desk and started back at writing down my notes. They spoke for about half an hour and the woman continued to be restless. Their conversation was low. At some point I heard her weep. I looked in the kitchen. My Mama was holding her in her arms. I could see that the woman had a large tattoo on her left forearm. There were tears in her eyes. She was ready to leave.

My Mama walked her over to the door, she put on her long coat and left. But, before leaving, she had transferred the stew into one of our pots and Mama washed her bowl, dried it with a towel and gave it back to her. My Mama came back and sat down at the dining table and she was quite angry. I know when my Mama is angry. Her ears get red and she looks down at the floor.

I walked in and asked, what was that all about, because the woman seemed a bit afraid. My Mama said, "Your grandfather is a bastard."

Outside our house I heard the Romani hawker's voice trailing off, "From dusk to dawn, from dusk to dawn."

Chapter Five

On August 23, 1939, German Foreign Minister Joachim von Ribbentrop stooped over a table in Moscow and signed a deal with Soviet Foreign Minister Vyacheslav Molotov, who was already sitting down under the watchful gaze of Ioseb Besarionisdze Jughashvili. It was immediately popularized as an alliance, which it was not. After failing to come to an agreement with the French and the English on how to deal with the Germans, and being increasingly concerned by the role of Japan on their eastern flank, the Soviets who had until then stayed out of the strife in Europe, decided to make a non-aggression deal with the Nazis. My grandfather was quite incensed. Bo thought that Stalin was being smart and buying time.

While the sound of the cratering bombs was relatively distant, the sense of terror unleashed on our town was not. It was an inescapable fact that the pounding sound was coming closer and closer. If the sound was hearable, I knew that it surely could not be too far away. But my mother suggested otherwise: not to worry. The mountains, said my Mama, magnified and reverberated the sounds of the bombs, spread it around and created unnecessary panic. As I realized much later, she was very practical. She had to manage the anxiety levels of the household, suppress her own concerns and the intermittent psychosis generated by a fitful grandfather. But I knew it was not the same. And there was also a build-up of tension that singed the insides of my mind, taught it to fight fear, stay calm and still embrace nervousness as a necessity. Because if you were not being nervous, you would be lying to yourself.

The church spires and mosque minarets trembled with empathy, while the sputtering sounds from exploding TNT from the forests beyond the mountains—far beyond, as I would say to myself—made for a comforting feeling. The partisans were practicing, my Mama would say! The Byzantine domes lost a few blue tiles, as they slid down and crashed on the steps all around them, as if a mischievous goblin perched on top of the dome was tossing ceramics down in different directions in acts of provocation or incitement. The birds panicked and flew around in clusters and took shelter in trees and then dived under the stone bridges, instead of hiding in the minarets and spires.

The discussions soon changed, the festive mood in the town subsided, the hawkers and peddlers in front of the courts and on the stone bridge started to thin out, the parade of religious festivals seemed to diminish and I could sense that my grandfather's repugnant and foreboding voice got louder and more powerful. He could now tell people he did not even know, what they should be doing with their lives. Artisans, farmers, lawyers, administrators, teachers, workers, cobblers, sausage and pastry makers all felt that he was in the know of things and therefore they had to somehow listen to his announcements as he tweaked his moustache and frowned at and pilloried the folks who had had rallies to fight the Axis powers. He made a big show of ripping up posters that were attached to the civil court's walls where his offices were situated. He stood on the stairs and told everyone off. Who was he against and who was he for? It was not that clear to me, yet.

Sometimes, he would drag me along and I know my mother would not be happy. When I told my Bo about what was going on, he was definitely annoyed and called his old man an idiot. At one lecture outside the steps to his office, he called for a new beginning for our country. He stated in clear terms that we had had too much freedom, too much tolerance for nonsense and too much intermixing. A new liberation was necessary.

The ambience in the markets changed, the level of voices amongst the people diminished considerably and a point was reached when whispers were the loudest sounds you could hear. People nodded at each other, rather than greet and shake hands or hug. The voices, the languages, the sounds were all put through silencers. The birds fluttered away but took shelter under the bridge. The current in the canal got stronger and I overheard that my grandfather was starting a new political party. My Bo seemed to know but did not want to talk about it.

While all this may seem like we lived in a little village of imbeciles, where the priest and the prosecutor ruled, the reality was that a much larger population stayed away from these public displays of their affiliations and went about living their lives, as they chose. And they did so with much deeper convictions, which allowed them to head off into the mountains to join the partisans or organize in the towns. Or, choose the option of being royalists.

***

It was around this time that my Bo recounted to me what he did with my grandfather when he was growing up. This was towards the beginning of the century—along the river, or perhaps the canal. I do not remember for sure, but he did talk about the stone bridge and therefore it must have been in the town itself, constructed by the Vazir Diedar, the vegetarian Muslim with a Buddhist streak, from many mountains beyond. The Vazir had spoken of his passion for peace and harmony and was described as the founder or harbinger of an era of tolerance. That sounded like something my grandfather would not tolerate! That is what my father said with a wry smile.

My father must have been in his teens and was a good swimmer, according to my grandfather. He could swim across the canal and back, several times in one go. They parked their boat, in the deepest section of the river, where sturgeon, trout and shad would congregate. My grandfather would pull out his double-barrel shotgun and blast away into the water and the shell-shocked fish would rise disoriented to the surface, and Bo would have to dive in and grab the fish and toss them into the boat. That to me required sound technique and stamina. I would have a hard time swimming in the canal, never mind trying to grab the fish in the river and then throw them into the boat. But my grandfather thought it was a great sport and while the family would need only a few fish for the day, my grandfather would insist on blasting away at the fish out of sheer, abominable, vindictive pleasure. My father, despite being tired, would be compelled to dive in and continue collecting the fish. My grandfather, would then toss out most of the dying or dead fish into the river and bring a big sack of gasping ones, back. Unknown to my grandfather and at the behest of my grandmother—who passed away at a very young age leaving my father with no siblings—my father would quietly go and distribute the still gasping fish to neighbours, who did not mind at all. They thought Bo was an angel, which he was.

It is these stories of my father's swimming aptitude and his secret pleasure in distributing the fish to neighbours and my grandfather's affinity for malevolent pleasure from utterly cruel behaviour, that gave me a good understanding of the evolving distance that separated my father from his father.

When they came back home from their misadventures in the canal—and this happened pretty much during the time that the great War was beginning to take shape—my father recounted how he had a hard time biting into the fish at dinner. There was a common kitchen then and there was only one house in the compound. So, my grandparents, my father and occasional relatives and friends dropped by to enjoy the fish, sausages, red cabbage stews and rip at bread made by my grandmother.

According to Bo, the first big War was not simply triggered by the assassination of the Austrian Duke, as is recounted in most history books. It was simply a convenient incident. Of that, later.

No wonder, a lot of nations did not wish to participate in that War. But to not participate in such a catastrophic war, where all nations used every form of toxic chemicals available, and then went on to gassing people and torching cities, was labelled as unpatriotic. Un-nationalism, as my father explained, was made synonymous with treachery and rapacious, bloody-minded brutality committed on fish in calm canal waters and was the psychotic need felt by unhinged barons.

Bo returned for two days and he looked terrible. For the first time I realized he had a greying beard, his face was drawn and his beret had lost its shape. He did not look tall and he did not stand as he did at the threshold, and my mother hardly spread out her warm smile and welcome. In fact, she did not smile at all. I had been sent off to a second cousin's house, further to the north of Sabzic, for a summer break. It was another small town along the river. Almost identical, except there was no canal that looped around this town. This second cousin from my mother's side was the same age as me and she was more excited that I was staying for a week than I was. I was missing Nika, my mother and her fantastic corn flour pastries. Why I was despatched there, was not known to me. I was desperately wanting to go back to our house. I was glad when school restarted. I had had enough of this dull-witted second cousin, who clung to me like a sloth.

I trudged back home from school on an indifferent day when the clouds moved about directionless. A nomad bead seller, sitting on the footsteps of the courthouse, held up a necklace to me with a cavernous, toothless smile. The winds were low or still, and my satchel of notebooks and books hung low on my back. The weight had been reduced because, while teachers in my high school insisted that all the books to be taught should be carried to the classes, I had realized in no time that the heavy books for Mathematics, Algebra, were not really required by the teacher. The teacher simply went to the black board and chalked up all that we needed to know for the day. We were expected to follow him on the board or copy down, only to find out that he was doing almost all the examples in the books, one by one. So, there was no need to carry the books, really. Some of the students in my class felt I was breaking the rules and was being reckless and looking for trouble. I felt I was being like Bo, unruffled, controlled and practical. Shaf had stopped coming for more than a month and strangely enough, Nika had gone off for a break somewhere, as well. I did not really know where she had gone. She was eighteen by now, not going to college, helping a friend run a small vegetable stall, and no one could tell her what to do or what to wear and what to eat. An arrangement I found quite unacceptable. Because no other families, that I knew, allowed their eighteen-year-old girls to go away on their own.

It made some sense to me that Shaf was not making regular appearances at our house. My school was irregular and some of the teachers were no longer available. My mum spoke softly to my father. Her eyes scanned the house for my whereabouts. In the mountains beyond, the Brownings kept up the erratic beat that warmed my mother's heart. Sometimes I could be lying on a couch like a chameleon, reading a book, unnoticeable. That was understandable, because often my mother had made shirts for me from left over material from cushion covers. When our eyes met, she would take my father away by tugging his jacket sleeves and going into the next room. The tone changes, the whispers, were accompanied with significant words that made sense to me off and on. If I was not training my ears carefully, I would have missed the fact that they had been talking about my vibrant and *indépendantiste* sister.

I was around ten years old. Despite the bombings around our capital city, I was allowed to bike around our town. My mother, in somewhat of a compromise, allowed me to take on this independence without much anxiety and simply said that I should stay away from church spires and mosque minarets, as in her opinion they would collapse at the slightest tremor, be it from under the earth or inflicted from the sky. It was puzzling and I wondered why she had not asked me to stay away from the courthouses and the town council buildings, which had roofs made of slates and tiles.

So, I biked around town, sweeping over the cobbled stone bridge, swerving out of the way of carts and cars till I reached the other side of the canal. Then I would rest on the southern side, away from the central town. It was predominantly the side of town where there were few churches although different communities were settled on both sides. The sun, setting slowly, would slip in and out through the green foliage and dazzle my eyes, as I pulled out a sausage sandwich from my rucksack. There were parts on this side of the canal, where the Strand was not that developed. The centuries-old stones made the Strand most attractive, and I would say a perfect place for young people to hold hands and kiss in the shadow of the embankment wall or walk along in the shade. And I preferred it because I would sit against the trunk of one of these trees, away from the noisier side, and eat mouthfuls of sausage sandwich.

I looked up at the sun, the sky and I knew that my mother would soon want me home. And on one of those tremendously satisfying ventures outside the pale-yellow walls of the compound we lived in, I looked away from the intermittent glare of the setting sun and saw, about ten trees away, a woman with a flowing black skirt that had a blue embroidered trim cozying up to a man, then sitting astride him. The man's hands held her around the waist. She looked at him in the eyes and lowered her lips to his.

On my way back, as I was crossing the bridge, I spotted my grandfather with a long telescope. At his side was his valet, the Serf—as he was better known to my parents. The Serf was looking away to another side, not interested with what my grandfather was focused on.

Chapter Six

As much as I enjoyed my high speed, bottom-jarring bike trips across the stone bridge, I also stopped, at times, in the middle. I leaned against the stone parapet and watched the river flow down below us. I also looked at the etchings done on the parapet that possibly went back a few centuries. With knives that had obviously cut some throats and severed arteries. Migrants, travelers, peddlers, soldiers, priests and conquerors had all stopped and looked down at the foamy swirls that formed eddies along the curves of the canal, where rocks and fallen branches formed an obstruction and provided such epicentres for reflection. The top of the parapet had a dirty brown colour from the thousands of elbows that had rubbed against it. That brown colouration allowed the knife wielders to scrape and carve their presence into the bridge as witness, for over a couple of centuries at least.

A relatively amicable relationship existed between the three main religions as well as those within the Christian fold who were Catholic or Orthodox, and between Muslims who had once perhaps been Manicheans or Zoroastrians, and people from the Caucasus who had adopted Judaism instead of being converted to Christianity or Islam. Their names and initials were engraved on the parapet. My father did explain one curious aspect of this country, which is that everyone over the centuries spoke a similar language with minor modifications here and there, but words from past empires were also incorporated. For example, Turkish words were quite prevalent and so were Greek and Italian words. Until then I had not known that some Muslims and Christians did intermarry and often lived together, because they spoke the same language.

The bridge had two towers on either side. Perhaps three floors high with a small observation deck on top.

"Quite irrelevant and useless, at this time," Bo would say, referring to the towers.

At the peak of the bombing and the eventual but quick collapse of our royal rulers, the swirls and eddies that remained in obscure corners of the canals were the only testimonials to a flow that was historic. Swirls that, Bo reflected, were like congregations, the embracement of intimate beliefs in each other's common history as speakers of languages intertwined, and even religions that sounded so similar. In our house there was never any mention of religion. No church, no mosque, no synagogue, no Bible, no Koran.

On one of these bike trips back from the bridge and the other side of town, I stopped at the little plaza in the centre of the town to drink some water. I was at a marble basinet situated on the side of a building which had a door with a recessed wrought iron grill on the top section. The water ran continuously from the mouth of a cherubic gargoyle. As I bent down to put my mouth in the stream, I heard an echoing voice in the plaza.

Someone was addressing a fairly large gathering. He stood on top of the courthouse stairs, while one of his underlings held a megaphone in front of his mouth. I could not get too close, since there was quite a large gathering in front of him. The voice echoed and bounced off the walls of the two big churches that sat opposite each other. I did not know what he was talking about, but his speaking skills were dramatic. He was not like a marionette or a joker. He spoke with poise, turning from one side of the crowd to the other. He paused and raised the palm of his hands and his fingers pointed to the mountains and, as well, to our town. He seemed to smile as he put his arms across his chest. He nodded and asked for acknowledgement and the crowd readily responded. "Do you agree?" he asked. The crowd roared. He did this several times. I went closer and closer to him. Later, he would get slightly agitated and his palm quickly transformed into a pointed finger. He seemed to be admonishing the crowd. I went closer and was able to hear some words, but I still could not make out the voice or the person.

"True blood, true blood! *Sangue vero!*" he said. His head started to swing from side to side in angry tones. The earlier poise was gone and, like an exorcist, he was on a roll. I could hear him say words that sounded like a variant of the language we spoke at home. And sometimes, I thought he spoke Italian words. I inched forward until I could get closer, near an obelisk that was at one corner of the plaza. I climbed up on the steps and put my bicycle to one side.

It was then that I realized who it was. He kept using a word that sounded like *rise up and burn!* in a language my mother also broke into often, but of course she used words in the most comforting manner when she used that language. A curiously parallel language, I would say. When I came down from my vantage point, I could not see my bicycle. It seemed to have been moved by somebody.

I kept pushing through the large gathering of men and some women, butting my head into the hips and chests of the excited crowd. I was unable to find it and my nervous sadness grew into a dark storm. The bicycle was not to be seen. I kept nudging my way around the obelisk. I returned to the drinking fountain, just in case I had left it there. My eyes welled up finally.

The walk back to the house took nearly forty-five minutes. I walked past the canal, looking back often just in case someone may have found my bike and would have recognized it. No such luck. My feet slithered pointlessly along and while I was not concerned that my parents would be upset, the loss of such a mode of transportation left me heartbroken.

I reached my Mama and told her about the bike. Not about the speaker. She understood and held me tight. There was no talk of a replacement. I did explain to her about the rally in the plaza and the words that were being used and my Mama seemed to know right away.

My lips quivered as I talked about the loss of the bicycle. She put her arms around me and the touch of her arms around my shoulders made me gasp with relief.

Chapter Seven

I had my chin down on the desk, pretending to be busy with my Algebra homework. My left hand held up my head, to one side. The school master would never have allowed that. But Shaf did not seem to care. I was disturbed and annoyed that in these earth-trembling times, the school master had to give homework. And I was nervous and uncertain that they may have seen me while they were in the shade of the tree at the south side of the canal. Did they? On the other hand, it was my grandfather who had the telescope and could also have seen me. I was not sure. Perhaps he was being a bit nonchalant about it. I had not seen Nika, since. I had gone to school early, only to find out that it had been cancelled but homework was duly allocated. Nika must have been sleeping.

Shaf had come in and parked himself on a couch, behind me. He was not much of an enforcer or overseer of my academic advancement. I was not looking at him. He was responsible, it seemed, to Bo and respectful of my Mama. At some point, she came in with a tray of sweet cheese fries. And biscuits, neatly arranged in a blue-and-red bone-china plate with gold paint around the rim. All set in a tarnished silver tray. There was a coffee mug with a long metal handle that she held with a cloth towel. The steam was coming out of it like a genie that appeared and disappeared, in circular coils. Shaf jumped up and Mama commanded him to sit down. Which he did. What a timid son of a bitch, I said to myself. It was only my Mama! You have not met my grandpa. She poured the coffee, which was so strong that it made him smile in delight. She lifted the mug up, just about two feet in the air, so the coffee landed in the glass and foamed up a bit. The glass had a tarnished holder attached to it.

He ingested the coffee and looked up at her, like he was breaking fast or something. My mum left.

I continued, balancing equations. L.H.S = R.H.S.

***

He was mumbling to himself. I pretended that I did not hear him. He had pulled out some papers from his satchel. He was writing stuff down on scraps of paper, as he often did, while making groaning sounds. Sometimes he ripped a page from his diary and tossed it into a wicker basket. Got to take a look at them, later. I turned around and looked at him. He smiled to himself pleasantly. He had come out of his spell and switched out of his groaning sounds.

"Writing episodes, like short stories," he said in a shy kind of way. "I am fixated by the character Poprischin, in Gogol's *Diary of a Madman*." He looked at me with a smile.

"Oh! I don't know much about this Poprisky guy!"

"Oh! You will, you will! Maybe in another ten years. There is nothing like the Russians, when it comes to beauty, honesty, meaninglessness and family." It took me around twenty years later to read *Crime and Punishment* and find *meaning* in what he said.

He went on and circled around the small room, in a merry and gleeful manner. There was a picture of a Russian aristocrat, or maybe a writer, standing up eloquently, with a pipe in his hand, in my parents' room. He had transformed himself into that. I no longer saw him as the leatherjacketed, bicycling, physics teacher. He seemed to have gotten an air about him. He gently put the coffee mug down and stared out the window.

The conversation had stopped and I showed him what I had done. From a distance, he looked at it for five seconds and said, "You got it!"

At that moment, a powerful wind rush accompanied by a soundless flash and followed closely by a rolling boom took over the room. The window in the kitchen rattled nearly to the edge of disintegration. My Mama rushed in. Shaf got up and looked through the window. It was like one single explosion.

"A mortar?"

There were no sounds after that.

"See you next week."

"Should you be leaving now?" My Mama seemed concerned.

He smiled.

"Its Ok. It is better a mortar from the ground than a bomb from the air."

He left quietly.

Nika rushed out from her room. She must have been sleeping.

"Did he leave?"

I picked up his diary. He had forgotten about it. I tucked it away, under a cushion, to read later, without Nika and my Mum knowing. He is going to come back for it, I said to myself.

I picked up a piece of the cheese fries and I went to the window. He was walking to the gate to his bicycle, which he normally tied to a post outside the compound wall. His satchel was hanging loosely. Did he not realize that the weight of the notebook was not there? My grandfather was under the portico, looking out into the sky. His thumbs were inside the waist pocket of his coat. He saw Shaf and his face turned to a spiteful grimace. But that was my opinion. My Mama may not have shared that.

Everyone seemed to know that he was seeing my big sister. Nika looked out from the front door. But he had already gone, that reader of Russian novels about beautiful madmen. Good in Physics, but probably better in History. He held my sister, who wore flowing black dresses with lace around the hem. He left when there was a boom in the sky and everyone trembled. Shaf had no family name. Was it a shortened name? Was he Christian or Jewish? Was he Muslim? Was he vegetarian? I did not ask and I did not know.

Chapter Eight

There was something that made me very uneasy and guilt-ridden about possessing something which did not belong to me. As an added complication, my curiosity about its contents was over the top. I remembered it created a pain in my lower abdomen as well as a rise of temperature in my head. These were manifestations of my nosiness and the suffering caused by my own wavering sense of morality or scruples.

I had kept the notebook under a big cushion in the small sitting area outside the dining room. The notebook had critical material or *stuff* in it, that was more than exciting. But quite a bit that I did not understand a word of. I had sneaked a few looks into it. There were sketches of various geometric shapes. Diagrams. Coordinates, as I learnt later. Sometimes there were mathematical clauses, with calculus signs as far as I understood. There were all sorts of densely written stories in there. I mean they could be stories or self-reflections. Or notes, from books. I had just stolen a few looks. This needed a lot of figuring out. I wanted to read it without my Mama or Nika catching me at it. I had carefully ensured that the cushion did not sit in a strange manner and attract any attention. I opened the notebook and laid it out flat. Nobody went in there, as the room was a bit cold. I figured that I had lost my bike and he had lost his notebook. There was some parity there. Could be useful.

Our country was at this point mostly occupied in sections along the borders, by various neighbouring nations. Some aligned with us, while others seized the opportunity to grab some territory, because our Kingdom was militarily unprepared. Within our country, there were those who aligned with the evil fellow in Berlin and were enthusiastic about ripping apart the idea of the social union this region had endured. They wanted it dismantled as fast as possible into small nations and others were simply interested in monarchy. But one could not deny that there was way too much conflict in the history of our confederation to hold together all the different language and ethnic groups by asserting the dominance of any one group.

Sabzic, despite my grandfather's determination to rename it as Goshtlow—which had not gained much momentum—remained an entity of its own. The waters in the canal remained translucent green. The air was fresh and clean. The trees along the sides of the canal, although still equally spaced, grew disproportionately, sometimes leaning over, not knowing which way to grow, but still there. A few had fallen and had not been removed from the canal. Several buildings closer to the edge of town, where the curving roads led up to the mountain, had been hit by stray gunfire. There were some skirmishes happening in the town. The stone bridge had lost its sheen, with the sharp edges chipping off here and there, while the rounded surfaces, remained in better shape, but darkened considerably. The town itself remained very much intact. The pale-yellow buildings reflected the sunlight at dusk as they always did.

Prayers were still being said in the churches, mosques and synagogues, while birds fluttered away from the top of the domes, on cue from the listless, nomad bead seller who threw scraps of bread on the steps around the city court and muttered incessantly from under a dark robe. People stopped and talked to each other. Different faiths sat down and shared coffee. Overall, the project was still working.

Being in the central part of the country, it had no ports, no airports, very few factories. But it was evident that the resistance had shaped up and partisans were hitting the various occupying forces and running away. That is the way to fight, said my Mama, a subdued smile on her lips. But I saw new faces in town. Rugged looking men and sometimes women, with pistols strapped to their hips. I was unable to go to the area of the Strand that I frequented. The walking took too long and my Mama was reluctant to let me go.

A devious strategy started to emerge in my head. I could tell Shaf that I had found his notebook and maybe he could loan me his bicycle from time to time, when he visited Nika. A puerile, infantile strategy indeed, as I realized much later, and was quite embarrassed about. My tuition schedule was now of secondary importance, as all had tacitly agreed. The bicycle was his major mode of transportation. He was quite particular about it. It was almost his lifeline. For me, the bike was a sort of anarchic liberation—freedom, of sorts. To pedal around madly, feel the breeze over the bridge, stand myself up with my legs straight down on the pedals and whiz in and out of the roads around the Strand and then go over the bridge, slow down and sit somewhere. If I got another bike, ever, I would tie it with a chain to my waist. For now, there was no chance of a bike. I would not even bring up the subject with my Bo when he reappeared. He had been away for more than two months, already.

Bo appeared finally and Shaf also turned up the very next day. They were in touch, obviously. The notebook was not part of the discussion. I found that rather mysterious and confounding. Did he not care about his writings and scribblings? Did he plant it purposely? Is he that forgetful and unattached to his possessions? As I was feeling kind of ravaged by these thoughts, a whistling sound was heard and immediately after a mortar landed somewhere nearby and the windows in my parent's bedroom vibrated for a while. Bo raised his head to look at Shaf, concerned. Shaf made a quick departure, despite my Mama trying to dissuade him.

Every time my mother asked him to stay for dinner, he apologized and stated that he had to go home. She did not press him too much. She accepted his excuses, whether they were valid or perhaps there was some other significance to it. Was it religious? Or did he have a nationalistic distance from our family? I had never heard my parents disclose their religion or language preferences. He had never brought up his either. They spoke in the same language, in the same way as I did with them. There were no adjustments. I remained astounded that he was not asking me about it. The diary. I had also rehearsed in my mind how I would disclose to everyone that I had found it. In fact, at times at night I could not sleep, because I would go over and over how I would broach the subject with him. I would have to make sure Nika was not around, because she would be most displeased and possibly fuming about it. But, more importantly, I wanted to read all of it before I gave it back.

***

77

I was eleven by the time the occupation of our country had been essentially completed and the Second World War was in full swing, but the resistance to the insane clown from Berlin (as my mother referred to him) and his various allies, was by now widespread. Shaf had been coming to our house for over a year. There had been weeks, before the bombing of our country had reached a peak, he would come to our house on weekends, he would play chess with my father if he happened to be around, eat my mother's tarts and pastries and the scorching coffee would be poured hot into glasses with a superbly steady hand from a couple of feet above, by who else but my Mama. If my mother asked him to stay for dinner, he would say, "Next time, for sure." So, my mother got fed up and stopped asking him. She even stared him down once when he was leaving. He took a curt bow, smiled and left. He must have realized. The next time he came, he brought a big pie. That was enough to make my mother furious.

"What is that all about, Shaf? I ask you to have dinner with us and you refuse each time. And now you bring a pie?"

He dipped his head.

"Sorry, ma'am. I made it. Thought you might like it."

My parents were embarrassed. But I knew, at his age, he could do things that most boys or men never bothered to even think about doing. We sat down together that night and had his pie. It was a minced beef and corn pie. He then informed us that it was called pâté chinois. It had nothing to do with Chinese cuisine, but that workers from Quebec, building the railroad across the big American country, had lunch served by Chinese cooks, hired and supervised by English bosses. So, they referred to it as Chinese pies. When the workers moved on to work on building railroads in Maine and Massachusetts, they spread the word as well that it was pâté chinois. And the tradition continued. We listened carefully and respectfully as he told us that night for the first time that his father was a railway worker, of part Turk and part Greek origins.

"My father got run over by a wagon train while trying to save a boy who had wandered on to the crossing. We were to join him, but it never happened." We had just finished the pie when he finished telling us his story.

My Bo seemed to know about it, as he kept his head down. The rest of us stared at Shaf with a silence that he perhaps could not comprehend. He did not mention much about his mother. But whenever they had this pie, his mother's eyes welled up, he said. She had learned to make it from the father.

He kept looking at me from across the table, as if he knew I had the notebook. My shoulders drooped from the disclosure about his father. Nika sat next to my mother and I sat across from him and next to my father. You know, to lose a father when you are young has got to be an immense and hurtful experience. And I looked at my father's hands as he had them entwined in front of him, as he looked up towards Shaf.

***

Sometimes, Shaf would ask that we go for a walk. My mother would readily agree. Because he was more than ten years older than I was.

My father said he was good in Physics. It was a subject I was destined to take in a few years time. When the War ended. He was impatient that I get an advanced grasp of it. I weighed the idea of listening to him and understanding

Physics, because he made it so stellar. So cosmic. As long as there was no bloody homework associated with it. But the Physics that I later came to comprehend was very much a subject that was rooted on earth and not in space or the cosmos. It was about electromagnetic forces, gravitation, atomic interactions, and if Shaf would have his way, there were the forces of ideas and intellect and lightspeed that would govern, bend opinions and emotions at a distance and change mindsets of nations and peoples.

We were walking in a lane behind the walls of a small auto repair garage. It was a dark evening with no street lamps around. The bombing had lessened and our country was now quartered, if not hung as well, into regions of occupation and guerilla resistance.

There were no shadows on the ground and I kept looking out for dog poop. Despite the darkness, he kept spinning a wooden top, which he carried in his satchel. He would swing it in the air, let it land on the palm of his hand and make it continue to spin till the rotation died out. He would wrap his fingers around it as it slowed down. He beamed and looked at me sideways. Not once would it land on the road. He would smile and then start wrapping the string around the top again. Every time I tried doing it in broad daylight, I would end up flinging the top into the air and it would fly out into an arc and simply land with a *thunk* and not spin at all. Either I did not know how to tie the string, or I did not know how to make that special wrist action that gave the top the required spin in the air.

When we sat down on a fence made of railroad ties, under a disconsolate, sooty lamp that hung outside the auto repair garage, he explained rotation/relativity/time space. I listened. Inside the shop I could hear rodents doing a wriggle-dance, squatting, nibbling and fidgeting till they had ingested enough wood shavings, metal chips and engine oil. Shaf heard them too and he waited for their silence and then he began.

"The top eventually loses its rotational velocity in time, not because it did not get enough of a spin to start out with. But because of time!" And he repeated the word *time* again, somewhat louder.

Mangy, unfed dogs howled from the end of the street, their eyes glowing in the dark. He stared back at them. He re-emphasized time, like I was not getting the point. He continued, while the dogs circled around and whimpered or growled.

"It is not because of friction, although friction does play an important role. Friction is obvious. The top has to stop spinning sometime, when observed. You know what I mean? Capeesh? There are two phenomena happening here!"

I liked the way he used the word *phenomena*. It automatically elevated the exchange to a very high level. We were not discussing ground level stuff, here.

"Gravity—" his one finger pointed downwards, "and observation —" he takes two fingers to his eyes.

"And both are governed by velocity. And velocity is...?"

"Velocity is speed over time," I murmured, knowing that no one in my grade had any clue about it and I was way ahead of them. "But I know it loses its speed."

"Yes, that too. Due to gravity."

"But what is gravity then?" I would get a bit confused. "A force from the centre of the earth?"

"Yes and no. All objects with inertia are subject to a space-time curve. Gravity is a natural force of attraction between any two objects that travel in time. Actually, it is the tug of time."

Now he had plugged in the word inertia and I needed to ask him later what it really meant.

"Tug? Like time is pulling at the wooden top? At an angle and making it slow down?"

He took a deep breath and spat out a gob which arced over to the other side of the lane. The dogs got up and moved away. He was silent, for a while. What distance separated his thoughts from my sense of comprehension!

"Everything is relative! Nothing is absolute. Time, distance. Everything! Everything that we measure is relative...except one thing! The velocity of light."

He stood up and stood still. I waited for him to say something.

"The velocity of the top can never approach the velocity of light. So, in a relativist sense, it is miniscule. So, the top must eventually stop spinning, just as an apple must fall to the ground. Just as our eyes wander and stop being fixated on something. Just as I fucking sometimes have no clue what I am talking about!" I could sense his frustration.

He scratched his head and stared at the dark mountain that rose beyond in the distance. He pulled out a cigarette from his pocket. It was half smoked. He lit it up. I came pretty close to understanding what TIME was, at that point. And without having a real inkling of Physics.

We started walking again and he started to talk about observations. Observations, like when you make a finding with your eyes and describe it. We walked back towards home.

Then the explosion happened. There was someone with heavy footsteps outside our door. Shaf and I had barely opened the main gate and stepped into the compound. The door was wrenched open and before my father could even get up, my grandfather Marcus, the public prosecutor from Hades, shoved aside the curtain and stepped in. Outside, in the hills, crackling machine gun fire warped into a piston-like a back-and-forth sound. Shaf had an idea. He asked me to go in and he mounted his bicycle and disappeared into the darkness. I stepped in and saw Nika was staring straight into my grandfather's eyes and he was sputtering from his mouth. A steady stream of unknown abuses came out of his hollowed-out mouth and hit us all, square in our jaws. He made no sense, but the vehemence was enough. I was not particularly scared. My mother stood up and my father stood in front of Marcus, with a show of defiance I had never seen. For every attempt made by him, my father's thundering voice—coming from nowhere—hit him back without letting him complete his sentences. As if he had prepared for this.

"And here I am trying to salve the nation's pride and honour…"

"Salve? Salve? Did you say salve? Which nation, what honour, which king are you trying to save? You are not going anywhere with your shit sermons. You are not achieving anything at all…"

"…and right here in my family…within the compound walls…"

"Yes, within these compound walls, we are living in this house, in peace. While a monster in Berlin wants to achieve his maniac dreams of a superior race ruling the world. And you are with him! Aren't you? I am asking you to leave. Now!"

"…my own granddaughter has chosen to sully our repu-tation, making everything mud! Mud! I say our roots, our religion, our language—by sleeping with…"

"What roots? What reputation? You are a collaborator! Just shut up and leave! You are killing Jews, Christians and Muslims! What beasts you are!"

With that explosion from Bo, I knew where the divide was. Darts were flying out of my mother's eyes. Nika's eyes were watery but she stood up straight.

I walked in and my mother pulled me away from the door. My Bo put his arms around Nika and told his father to leave.

"Immediately!"

The piston like back-and-forth sputtering sounds of machine guns got louder. Then came the heavy guns. It was no longer mortars, but also howitzers and field guns. My grandfather attempted to make a comeback and my Bo took care of that.

"Get out now!"

The old lawyer turned enforcer had begun to lose some of his dour charisma. He turned around and left. My Mama went and banged the outer door shut, with some vehemence.

My Bo was soon packing his bags. Substantially bigger than his usual satchels and briefcases. These were heavier and unwieldy. He wore bigger boots than before and thick jackets with a lot of pockets. He was often distracted and perhaps distraught. He was simply fuming, silently. That was what I felt.

Chapter Nine

My school finally closed its door, without a whimper and until further notice. The building's exterior was embraced by four red-brick stripes that ran along its entire two-storied, yellowish-coloured stone facade. The yard in front was well maintained. No blemishes, no damage to the wrought-iron railings along the perimeter.

While Sabzic was never bombed directly from the air, there were skirmishes happening outside the valley. Gunfire could be heard louder, and clearer, from beyond the mountains. There was evidence of stray gunfire inside the town as well. My mother was no longer insistent that it was far away. The steady build up of war sounds had allowed me to get acclimatized and it was like a sporadic drumbeat, at night. One of the things I realized was that since our family was living inside a walled compound, the possibility of stray bullets coming through the window was remote. However, if there was a stray shell, there would be no escape. This facilitated a developed level of complacency, and as well, a need for careful self-confinement. For the first time my mother started putting adhesive tape on the windows.

My grandfather was busy with his vituperative sermons in front of the courthouse steps, but his audience was dwindling. The malice in his blood was more than one could bear. He was critical of everyone who was not of a certain religious heritage that he was favourable to. And along with it, there was a fawning adulation for making speeches that seemed to sound like the leader of Italy, Benito—who had a rapid fire, staccato style of delivering speeches, swinging his head from side to side, supposedly from balconies, but we only heard his voice through a crackling radio my father had brought back on one of his trips. Even the Serf who picked up his valise and opened the door for him was no longer standing at attention and erect. He held the elbow of one arm with the other hand at his back. Dreariness showed. He looked away, as his backbone had kind of slumped, while my grandfather got into the phaeton and proceeded with his Napoleonic strut.

Nika and I seemed to have developed an affinity that overcame our sibling disregard for each other. We needed to overcome the unstated distancing she displayed with me. It was an artificially constructed superiority. With the ugly tension caused by my grandfather when he stepped into our house for the first time, and the sounds in the valley that suggested a nearing calamity, Nika chose to stay more at home. At this time, I realized that I would not see Shaf any longer. As it was, he was a paradox, but more importantly he was also an eccentric. My sister understood my affinity for Shaf and that brought her closer to me.

She lived in a state of contained panic though, never leaving the house, and if she wanted anything done outside, she would use my resources. She would read a lot of books, lying down on her bed. I would continue to spend time with the diary, in the bathroom or by the Strand, reading page after page of utterly baffling and confusing stuff, which required enormous concentration. There was no point in glossing over these pages, just because I could not comprehend it or because I wanted to move on to other issues. Each and every paragraph needed to be understood. What an astounding collection of thoughts! And I could not dog-ear them and that posed some difficulty, especially if I had not read it for a week or so. But I read with so much concentration, when I did, that I did not need a page marker. But my eyes did hurt.

There was a continuity that seemed to be running through one chapter and leading on to another. Sometimes it was about Physics and at other times it was about observations and the fact that observations were almost an idea conceived at a certain space in time, the observations themselves could not be the absolute truth. In fact, there was no absolute truth, except the transience and disorder at the core of all truths. His words. Like truth was a temporary conclusion or understanding on the chaotic disorderly conduct that our world was going through.

Did my grandfather make sense? Did he really believe in the governance of a nation by the beliefs of a single religion or language? And why were there such invocations of violence, military threats to separate nations that had pretty much lived comfortably together despite occupation, conversions and decades and centuries of conquests that attempted to obliterate the past, but could not? The idea of imposing an absolute truth, seemed suddenly like a weak and rickety marionette making threatening postures in a nervous manner.

The greenery around the Strand remained resplendent, and the skies were not grey. But on the ground, there was early darkness, as lights along the bridge and the canal were turned off. The radio crackled out news from both sides, but my Mama was exemplary in the sense that she was able to tune the radio to a rather intriguing broadcast from enemy territory. It was probably a caricature that my grandfather would have been attracted to. An American, who had spent most of his life in Britain and was a Nazi sympathizer, had fled to Berlin and was doing broadcasts in clipped intonations and rhetorical flourishes, taunting the British war effort. He was openly threatening the English with dire consequences on behalf of the Luftwaffe. It was then that I realized that once before, when I was inside his house, he was listening to this same voice in a tentative fashion and although he understood very little English, he was chuckling and chortling at the taunts. Years later when I was done with school, I came to know that this turncoat was executed in England after the War was over. But, for sure, he had left a mark on my grandfather's dreadful soul.

It took me more than half an hour to walk to the centre of the town. It was a relatively warm day. Then I crossed the stone bridge and spent another half-hour till I reached the house where Shaf lived with his mother. I was delivering a letter from Nika. I must have been exhausted and it showed. She was happy to see me—because we had never met before. I handed her the letter. And was about to turn around and leave when she stopped me and said, "Wait!"

She came back to the door with a meat pie, the famous pâté chinois, packed in a paper bag. And before I could even open my mouth—

"I know, I know—what you are thinking. There is something Shaf left behind for you, as well."

She went back to the yard at the side of the cottage they lived in and very soon came out rolling the bicycle.

"He said to give this to you, as he was not going to use it anymore."

I was moved and was speechless. My lips were trembling. What was on his mind when he decided that I could have the bicycle. Was he going away somewhere? That was his only means of transport. Why would he give it to me? Does he have no one else to give it to, in case he was going somewhere? Is it because he loved my sister and so that was his reason?

"Oh! How can I take this and the pie?" I managed to blurt out.

"Well, you put the pie in the basket in front and pedal away like crazy till you reach home and then you have the pie!" I had meant that I was taking two things back and I had delivered only one letter.

She was simply cheerful, with her one hand on her hip and with her eyes telling me to smarten up. I managed to say, "Thank you," in a manner that embarrassed me for my lack of composure and lexis. My throat was caught, my tongue felt like a slab of meat had died inside my mouth. I stammered somewhat.

"But, have you heard from him? Where is he now?"

"No, I have not heard from him in a while." Her eyes were not dry. That I could see.

"Do you know if he is working?"

"He had a job, teaching in a small college. But they let him go, because he was telling stories about the Italian Renaissance and not teaching Applied Physics, as he was hired to. Can you imagine!"

"So, they fired him?"

"I don't know. He told me he was going trekking somewhere in the north. I know he was lying. He has not contacted me for several weeks now. I was expecting a telegram at least. Don't worry, he will appear at some point and I will give him the note from your sister."

That would be a knock-out punch for Nika if she found out that he had taken off without telling her. I had seen them once earlier on, outside a tavern, a month after the bark-howl-bite act carried out by my grandfather in our house. They sat together and smiled. He seemed quite unsettled and he scratched his head incessantly, like his appearance was of no consequence and she would keep grabbing his hand and forcing it down. Then she put her arms around him and he brought her closer to him by wrapping both his arms around her. I felt good, but also mischievous, that I had closer working knowledge of their romance than anyone else.

I thanked Shaf's mother, again. She was tall. Her head and ears were covered in a short black shawl. Her face was warm and craggy, though, like experience and age had produced a sculpture on a rock face. I regained my composure and kept thanking her with many syllabled words, and eventually took off down the road on the bike, with the pie in the basket. The smell from the pie was so strong and delicious that when I reached the bridge, I did not carry on towards home. I went under the bridge and sat down at a bench and devoured half of it. It did not escape me that he had satisfied my need for a bike, while I was in illegal possession of his prized notebook. I smiled and mounted the bike again, with half-a-pie in the basket.

Years later, when I was out of the country, studying, I realized that the bike had been my salvation in so many ways. I could do things that my mother and sister could not rush off and accomplish. I was free to travel to various parts of Sabzic, which they had probably never visited. One thing I clearly understood: mobility and aloofness were key to concentrating the mind. It was impossible to have your ideas solidify unless you could massage your thoughts alone, and without the distraction of sounds that were the result of the disturbances of living within four walls. Or, for that matter, being in an open space that had crowds congregating and chit-chatting loudly. The bike allowed for some significant zig-zagging. Weaving in and out of dense air and dense polemics.

Chapter Ten

Carrying a burden of ideas that were difficult to bear alone, I was on the verge of talking to my Mama, but at the last moment I backed away. I did not know how to begin. It was the confiscated diary that was killing me, actually.

I despaired at the fact that I was two goals ahead of him, as one would say in football, 2–0. I had his notebook and then I was in possession of his bicycle. He seemed uninterested in recovering the book and that really intrigued me. He was playing a game, but not by the rules. I had taken illegal possession of the diary for too long and the business of taking sneaking looks into it compounded my sense of shame. It not only made me feel guilty, but I felt deeply burdened. If I had wanted, I would have shared this knowledge with Nika, but I chose not to, because I had a feeling that she would have a fit that I had been sneaking into his private notes. Then she might just want to take a look herself and that would compound matters further, because I did not have a clear idea of what else was in it. Maybe some heartbreaking notes about her. That would be catastrophic.

I loved my sister in a special way. I did not think she understood that. She saw me as some sort of a baby. As I grew older, she saw me as both a troubled boy and perhaps a useful nerd. Her personality was not necessarily of an imposing or commanding nature, nor did she seem inquisitive like me. She was outgoing, but lived in a world of her own. I had never seen her conversing with my parents in the way I did. I did not know what she felt about the War that was going on, about my grandfather's growing arrogance, about the compound walls that were slowly falling apart, revealing mural by mural, much of our nation's historical transitions. Then there was the appearance and disappearance of our Bo. All this, I did not discuss with my sister and I felt quite torn and sad that the one who was supposed to be closest to me had no affiliation for me. Yet, I felt that she was also up to something, that she also had her own plans, that she had her own associations and that is why she disappeared from time to time and never told me where she was going.

At a certain point I found something very interesting on her desk. She was reading a book about the Krupp industrial family in Germany. It was heavily marked up, with underlined sections and exclamation marks. It was about how the Krupp group had become integral to Germany's quest to be a dominating nation in Europe, if not globally. It had been presented to her by, who else but, Prof. Shaf of course. One of the main chapters in it was on the Berlin-Baghdad railway line.

The British, wrote Shaf on the margins of the book, had their big guns stationed at the Suez. The Germans knew that oil and gas was going to define the next era. So, they were planning an alternate route to bypass the British areas of control.

"The first big War? A concoction! The Germans needed an excuse," says Prof. Shaf in one of his notes.

She had written a big "WHAT!" on the margin.

"What was the assassination of Franz Ferdinand all about?" she had asked.

"A ploy!" said Shaf in the margins again.

Later on, in his diary, I found a note about the assassination. He wrote, "A ragtag band of self-described revolutionists decided to bomb and then shoot the Duke as his unusual cavalcade snaked through a densely populated section of the city, without any security whatsoever. Strange is it not? The entire police force was practically absent that day and the magistrates and investigators obtained a rather quick confession from the mostly teenage assassins and promptly the War was declared. The case was closed."

Shaf and Nika were communicating on all these issues. They were together in discovering a lot of issues that they felt strongly about. I felt good, but also slightly left out, I suppose. It was a surprise and a let down that Shaf did not discuss such issues with me as he did with my sister. Like, I was okay for discussing velocity, BODMAS rules, observation and stuff like that. But, Bo, Shaf and Nika talked separately about ports, land routes, coups, Kings, Vazirs and cannons.

There was no sadness ever on Nika's face. Her smile was resplendent. The clear green waters of the river that snaked through our town, that she stared at often, were translucent and assertive, like her. There was no hesitation in her. She moved along like the ripples in the canal, in the current. She came to firm conclusions and went about her life based on them. But unlike me, she did not care to notice that the Serf's spine had slumped, that he was no longer the ramrod manservant and that his mind was probably made up. She did not see the tears streaming down the face of my grandfather's maid. She was preoccupied with thoughts of a more long-term nature, while I observed the ground-level changes, through cracks and half-opened bathroom windows. Naturally, she was in college and her exposure to international intrigue was deeper. I sat by the riverbank or observed things at the plaza and I looked at faces, clothes, knees, shoes and jackets of different nationalities and was able to decipher who was proud and who was unsure and afraid. I noticed my mother's sadness and occasional anger. Nika did not. But, I must say that as the years went by, I began to understand what my Bo often referred to as the "larger picture."

I did realize that when I fell asleep or pretended to, I could hear my parents and her having pretty intense discussions. My sister was quite adamant about her positions. She would not suffer the self-appointed baron any longer. She knew where he was coming from. That he was being intolerant towards Shaf was merely a secondary issue, even a facade. It was an ethnic thing. That it really came down to a *German problem* in our lives, at that time. I listened and marvelled that she had such clear ideas, that I had only grasped years later. I did not understand the complex nature of the problem until the Germans started their Blitzkrieg and smoke started coming out of chimneys in lands occupied by them. In fact, one of the other things I realized was that the world outside only keeps talking about the latest massacre that happens and erases the memories of the previous massacres. So, a few decades go by before we unearth the past brutalities of one community against another and the reason behind the lingering hatred. The latest acts of brutality take centre stage and past brutalities get erased.

As a consequence, and as a result of such confounding understandings of historical events, I felt that I must stop trying to form solid opinions about every event that I came to know of and I took the firm decision to return the diary. Because its presence in my hands was not only becoming too much of a burden, but it was prolonging my ability, at my age, to come to firm conclusions.

I was hoping that Shaf would be there when I went to drop it off. In fact, no one was there. Not even his mother. I circled the house and looked into the back window, leery that some neighbour was possibly watching me. I sneaked to the side of the house, where the bicycle had been parked before. There was a porch on that side. And a rocking chair with a small table sat on the wooden patio. I had brought the diary wrapped in a paper bag. I looked up at the roof and saw it was well covered and the chances of rainwater leaking in would be minimal. I placed the bag on the table and figured Shaf or his mother would see it for sure, because it was just next to the kitchen door. My disappointment in not seeing Shaf or his mother was total. It was not simply a question of discomfort from an unsuccessful attempt at cleansing my mind of the shame I bore, but I had prepared and gone over a speech to lay myself bare and retrieve my self-esteem.

I also chose to believe that if he was really out trekking, maybe he was not in love with Nika. After that horrible encounter with my grandfather, I had felt that he would think it appropriate to come and see her. But he did not and he went off trekking! That is how I understood things, plain and simple. I remained partly convinced that their love could be a fleeting romance. But I could not discuss this with her, my Mama or my Bo. And in the weeks that followed the flare-up in our house, and following which my Bo left for a long trip, I decided to make another visit to

Shaf's house, to see what he was up to. If he had come back and was still planning to get back to teaching. After all, I had delivered a letter for him from Nika, and now I had delivered back the diary, so it was okay to do a follow-up. Plus, I was deeply concerned that his monumental writings on Physics and Philosophy and banks and industries and railways and empires was not carried away by rats and other vermin from the side porch.

Chapter Eleven

I biked again towards the bridge to cross the canal at an easy pace. I looked down and saw the water rolling along as well, chattering self-consciously. These waters were witness to Vazirs, and before them Princes, Dukes and Barons, as they built their empires or sought the destruction of others; or when they were leisurely lying down on rugs or thrones, listening to music, gobbling imported plums, apples and oranges. The peace of mind these thoughts generated was, I would say, weighty. It was something I preferred over the immediacy of the booming sounds in the mountains, the hum of the bombers in the skies at night and the darkness in the town as the sun slipped below the horizon. My recent findings in the book Nika had been reading and the corresponding notes in Shaf's diary had left me quite preoccupied.

On June 10, 1942, one hundred and seventy-three men from the village of Lidice in the Czech Republic who were over 15 years of age were rounded up and executed, as reprisal for the assassination of Reinhard Heydrich, the Reich protector. I had turned twelve.

As I passed the plaza in the center of the town, I heard a frightening commotion in the distance and it built up into a roar. My ears had gotten used to hearing the steady tympanic sound of bombs falling in the distance, the stuttering of sten guns, like percussion in the hills beyond. It had the texture of an orchestra. There was grimness, but aloofness—even a sense of dignity. Like a Straussian symphony in the woods. Perhaps a bit light-hearted at times, but elevating at others. I had gotten used to it and I actually enjoyed listening to it.

But then came this uncompromising cacophony of baying wolves and cackling geese—rising to screeching and riotous shrieking, like blunt saws going back and forth on rusted pipes. From the majestic "Blue Danube," which my mother played so often on an old gramophone, the sound had now been reduced to that of a chaotic and delirious marching band that used milk cans and chattering teeth, for sound effects, while ghouls danced around each other on the cobblestoned plaza.

I stopped for a while and turned around to look. I could make out some nasty heckling, shouting of slogans to kill, to burn, burn and tear apart. Quite a melee was about to happen on the canal. I came closer to the bridge and saw in the distance that a figure wearing a long military style coat had assembled a rag tag bunch of hoodlums and grim-looking characters, who had lit torches in their hands and were obviously furious and ready to stomp on anyone who opposed their views in the plaza.

Something was headed in the wrong direction. The sun had nearly set and the anger was burning out of their eyes and licking out like flames, as they were kicking their feet and holding up their torches and probably planning to cross the bridge. My Bo would have been stomping his feet as well if he saw this. These hoodlums my grandfather had assembled spoke the same language as us, but there seemed to be a religious frenzy in them.

I followed them at a distance. As they crossed over to the other side of the town, their torches and crosses seemed like trees were on fire. I noticed, however, that a lone figure was coming back. He was swaying from side to side and seemed quite agitated, talking to himself and as well shouting to others who had assembled in various parts of the bridge. The Serf who had carried his valise and had opened the door for him every morning, was fuming and muttering as he came back down the bridge. He was not going along, it seemed. He had reversed direction.

The bridge was a turning point, like it had been, for several centuries. The stones, the two watchtowers on either side, stood like sentinels. Watching over the seething tension between the Orthodox and Catholics on one side, and the Muslims and others who were just floundering around on the other. The bridge that was built to cross over, and took more than a century to build, was now being used to reverse back. For the forces at war elsewhere, it did not matter who built the bridge and why! It needed to be brought down.

"That is it! That is it!" he kept muttering to himself. "I am done! We were all one, now we will be many and not one! We are done!"

He saw me and hesitated a bit, but I did not think that he was entirely sure it was me. I had not seen him for quite a while. He was going back to town. But that last phrase from him, registered deeply in the years to come—we were all one, now we will be many.

The hoodlums marched over the bridge. Once they reached the other side, they went on a quick trot, and headed along the banks. I had stepped aside and parked my bike under a tree. I stayed on the bridge, as it afforded a better view of the mob. They kneaded their way past many houses then moved swiftly in a direction that had me deeply concerned.

As their sound faded away, I felt less concerned and so I sat down under a tree, away from the bridge, and waited for the mob to come back, perhaps.

I took out a sausage sandwich that I had brought along, and slowly started biting into it. The air felt fresh and the sky was quite blue and, as always, the canal water was translucent green and in self-conversation. I stared at the houses on the northern side of the bridge. They seemed to have recovered somewhat from the machine gun fire that was exchanged a few weeks ago. Some internal sympathizers of the clown from Berlin had realized that our country was better off being with the Germans and the Italians rather than having a nation of our own. In their hurry, they had aligned and formed some groups that actually assisted the Italian forces that were not doing too well, themselves.

On the southern side, the houses remained untouched, except for the noise that was now fading away as the mob went further and deeper in that direction. I was happy that school had officially closed and my mother was relieved that my apathy for the sciences was not becoming such a bothersome issue. My mother was however strangely concerned that I was drifting away from liking Algebra, Trigonometry and some very rudimentary Chemistry, as taught under the guise of general sciences. My Bo on the other hand, was okay that I found interest in subjects other than science.

The wind had picked up as I finished the last bite of my sandwich and I got up and turned around to make sure my bike was still resting against the tree. I looked up and saw plumes of black smoke rising in the distance at several points along the small hill, preceding the mountain that lay beyond. A strange odor had started to drift in.

I looked further and saw that there were more plumes rising from different points. I had not heard any explosions or gunfire and yet it seemed in the distance that a battle was going on. After a few minutes I got a strong whiff of a smell that I would never forget the rest of my life. It was not wood, not plastic, not paper, not curtains, nor food being cooked.

Very soon after, the angry mob arrived back at the bridge. My grandfather was nowhere to be seen. Their numbers had grown and their roar was resounding in the whole valley, whereas the river flowed with such purpose, so peacefully.

I waited for them to pass and I started pedalling. As I came closer to the area where Shaf's house was located, I realized that paper and ash were flying around and the odour had reached a disturbing intensity. When I did finally reach the corner of the block where their house was located, I realized that it was all gone. Three houses were burning and there were some families sitting down on the pavement, weeping and holding themselves, staring at their homes. The women all had their heads covered, and the children clung to them. There were no young men around. Some old men sat on the road weeping. Another old man with a bent back was carting his belongings in a wheelbarrow. He was not crying. I reached their house and saw the flames had devoured most of it. The front roof had collapsed and there were no windows left. They had been smashed. I came closer and closer, looking in to see if anyone was still in there or if Shaf and his mother had escaped. There was not a soul anywhere. The sun had finally set and while little flames still licked the wood boards on the side of the ceiling and on the floor, I decided to step in slowly.

She lay there, bloodied, mangled, burnt—but her face was hers and, in her hand, she gripped a shovel. Her dry parched mouth and darkened lips were tight and shut. I could only see the black lips of Shaf's mum all the way home. It was unforgettable. The resolve in her wrists, as she gripped the shovel. The mother of pâté chinois, the wife of a railroad worker who had left for the US and was expected to bring the whole family over; the mother of Shaf, the inscrutable tuition giver. All in one, she lay there ignited, blackened, incinerated and with Shaf nowhere nearby.

Honestly, he was a very strange man, brilliant or not; he was always drifting from strange expressions to strange disappearances. What was he made of? Was he stable? Was he honest? Was he possessed? Did he have courage to face the world he had himself chosen to live in? And now his house and his mother had been burnt to the ground. He was nowhere to be seen.

I had no idea of what was going on, except that my grandfather was a criminal and created divisions in the city, in the neighbourhood and within the compound walls of our home. He had ripped apart a sense of community that I felt was natural to our town. He had stoked some flames that perhaps lay below the surface, and had never really mattered to most of its citizens. But that is where I felt things went wrong. Those hidden animosities, hostilities that come about from sheer mistrust, suspicions and even a sense of fear about the ways of others, had now been excavated, pulled out from the devil's cauldron.

Years later while in college, I realized that what was once a nation could fall apart and be divided into tranches of feuding tribes that had tolerated each other for nearly five hundred years. Of course, there had been conflicts, assassinations and battles that even triggered the big wars. And of course, countries had changed borders and maps were redrawn, but there was some reason to believe that there was a common heritage that could keep the federation glued together.

Could you also imagine that suddenly an entire tribe living on one side of a canal and going to a particular church became proselytizers for a particular socioeconomic belief system, while those on the other side of the canal, vehemently opposed it? And they had fought together as partisans? Well, that is what happened.

As I imagined, the diary, if it had not become ashes, would be flipping its pages in the wind as a record of some passing fancy, as the Allies landed in Normandy, V2 rockets started flying overhead at a thousand kilometres per hour, and one by one the clown in Berlin and his allies were ditching their posts in Rome, Athens, Paris, Warsaw while the Soviets pincered in from the eastern flank. My Bo, I realized, was no longer an aspirant for a medical career—perhaps he never was but was really an armed partisan.

While outside I heard cries and screams, inside, the diminutive flutter of flames within charred remains died with the sunset. The porch had been burnt down, the table and the rocking chair were a heap of ashes on the ground and the corpse of the nation had melted down. I shivered as I raced the bike back home.

The diary was history, I thought.

Chapter Twelve

The Serf was a Franciscan. Another faith that confounded me and compounded my inability to comprehend why disagreement and dissent must end up in dissection. If the intent was to spread the glory of Jesus in a civil manner, why not simply billet-out the preaching of it in a planned manner in different geographical territories? Allow for the church to spread its theology, as per local adjustments. Christians, Orthodox or Roman, had their anger simmering underneath; decency required that everyone smile pleasantly, hold hands, embrace each other, while they kept their knives sharpened. Why? Because Orthodoxy was dissimilar from the Hungarian to the Greek brand and for that matter any Slavic version. So, the key issue was—nationality. And once you raised your flag, you aligned with either the ruling junta or propertied classes and its Kings and Barons of the same nationality. My parents had no time for any religion or any flag. And that deeply influenced me.

I never asked him his name and he referred to himself as "the Serf" because both my father and mother referred to him as one, with significant contempt. There was clever and crafty humour in his taking up this derogatory reference to himself as his own badge of honour. His back up straight, but his eyes always focused on the gravel below, he jumped out and opened the door for my grandfather, then scurried away to pick up his briefcase.

I caught up with him, mumbling to himself at the water fountain in the plaza where my bicycle got pilfered. He was washing his face and his face was dark and perhaps bleeding a bit from above the eyebrows. He was attempting to disappear, but I was brisk, pedalling furiously, and I nearly crashed into him at the end of the plaza. He said good evening, without looking me in the eye. I asked him "Why?" He may have thought that I was questioning his greeting, but he was an intelligent Serf. He quickly realized I was asking him why Shaf's house had been burnt down and his mother had been murdered?

He sat down on the steps to the plaza and told me the whole story.

***

The phaeton had slowed down at the southwest corner of the plaza. Nika was lying on one of the stone parapets. Her skirt was flying up in the cool breeze and Shaf was caressing her face and had his other arm around her waist. The sun had nearly set and her profile was lit up like a reclining goddess. His words.

"Pardon me, Mr. Ben! Something must have gotten into his head. Something that made him very angry. I have known your father and your mother and while I am uneducated, my family is sworn to poverty and simplicity. I do know that in your family there is a lot of good intelligent people. But I have worked for your grandfather now for five years, and while I did my duty as required of me, I also knew in no time that he is Satan himself. Pardon me! I do not care for my job anymore. He saw the two of them and asked the coachman to stop. He looked at them for a while longer and that is when your teacher decided that he must do the unthinkable. He lifted her up and she sat up on the parapet and she put her legs around him, while their tongues flickered inside each other's mouths. Pardon me, again! You will excuse me, Mr. Ben, but your grandfather was also licking his lips, sweating and muttering unspeakable words. Then suddenly, he asked the coachman to "Move!" And the teacher heard it and turned around and smiled at him, like a fox, who had a rabbit in his mouth. That is how I saw the whole thing. Because I have worked as a trapper, as well, you know. And I don't know what your grandfather saw, but I sat facing him and can tell you that it was not just anger and disgust—it was like his soul was on fire."

"Are you Muslim?" I asked.

"God forbid, I am but Franciscan."

"So, can you tell me why the houses were burnt down?"

"Maybe, because there were some Turkmen houses in that area—not all, at least that is what your grandfather said. But I think it was a little bit personal, if you know what I mean."

"So, he thought he was protecting my sister?"

"Maybe, but it was a little more than that. I think he was envious, as well. I am very sorry Mr. Ben; I have to go. I am done with the prosecutor."

Nika was wild, but Shaf was like a prancing horse at one time, and a monk in a monastery, the next. The Franciscan Serf, however, seemed like he was transforming himself into a non-partisan partisan! He was in a rush and wanted the job done, it seemed.

Chapter Thirteen

On November 24, 1942, the Soviet Red Army had surrounded the Germans around Stalingrad. This was a turning point, because elsewhere, whether in North Africa, in the Pacific and even in Australia, Adolphus from Berlin and his Axis buddies were beginning to see their end. The writing was in the skies. But the action was on the cold ground below. The Japanese, after their initial successes in Singapore, were also backing away slowly, from what I gathered. They were quite intimidated.

Before I reached home, I picked up a newspaper from the plaza where my grandfather had trotted around with his numbskull confreres only a few months ago. I put the newspaper in my basket and whistled on towards home. I had crossed the bridge back and forth several times in the past few weeks. This time, the bridge was deserted. The wind was cutting into my face as I went through the Strand and over to the bridge. In the distance I could see huddles of people assembled around the carriageways of old buildings. They felt protected from the skies and stray gunfire. I felt deserted, left behind, as the wind sliced into me. No one was sitting on the steps leading up to the court-house and no one seemed to hang around the steps to the

Strand, except the indefatigable and listless Romani. They had no customers, no shelter—so they waved at me. I was somehow not quite conscious of what a stray bullet could do or, for that matter, a blast from a shotgun. In the eyes of the Romani, I saw confidence. The confidence they got from being pushed around continuously. They had become unwary of wariness.

When I reached home, I realized that something was incorrect. The gate to the compound was open and as I cycled in over the gravel, I saw my mother rushing in to stand in front of our main door. She was tearful and she raced towards me, hands flailing. Before I could go anywhere near entering the house, she stopped me and asked me to turn around and go to the house of a cousin who lived a little way up in the mountain. I was quite stunned and kept asking her, "What happened? Is Bo back? Where is Nika?" She kept pushing me towards the gate.

And for the first time, Lana Ester screamed at me quite unintelligibly and hysterically. It would have been an understatement to say that she had popped her cork.

"Listen to me...just turn back...do not ask questions, just do as I say and bike back to your cousin's house! Do not ask questions! She is waiting for you." Her voice broke, her throat went totally harsh and tears streamed down her cheek. She was weeping and screaming.

I stumbled out irritated, bewildered, and angry. I knew something had happened and that my Mama was out of control and would not let me in on what was going on. Lana Ester's behaviour was so gripping and compelling that I felt I must comply, just to reduce the level of tension that was really soaring up into the sky. I had never seen her like this. Had my father died?

I was imprisoned, like an idiot, for several days at the house of the cousin—who had no clue as to how to handle my confusion and was not forthcoming about any details. She only fed me and gave me a place to sleep. And I kept prodding her.

"What was the problem? Why should I listen to you and stay here? Why?"

She had no answer. Her head was lowered and she would say "I do not know, but you need to stay here. Please!"

She had a phone that she kept on a shelf on the wall and I could make out that she was talking to my Mama or possibly my Bo, softly. The nearly inaudible conversation was like a throbbing gong that kept reverberating in the ear for years.

"He...restless. He...Questions...but also listens. No... he has no clue."

Those were the snippets of conversation I could make out. My cousin, a docile and serious schoolteacher, had never come to our house, but my parents would talk to her often on the phone and would go over there as well. She lived with another woman, who was older than her and a socialist. They were lovers, my mother had curtly informed me, before I asked too many questions about their living arrangements.

This contrived secretiveness should not have happened, because there was always a natural exchange of ideas within the walls of our house. Nothing was really a secret. At least that is what I held close to my heart. The confidence level on the rights of individuals in the family to exercise an independent opinion was seen as supreme. The idea was always to consult each other, even an early teenager like me. There was only one occasion when I had exercised a certain departure from the family's unstated adherence to absolute truth. That occasion was when I chose to be reclusive and deny the accidental deposition of Shaf's diary on one of our couches at home. That had made me suffer interminably.

If I did not understand some statement that my parents made, I would bluntly pose a question and both my parents would explain, with great care. It was unheard of that I would be pushed out and asked to leave my own place of comfort, without any explanation. It was an insulting expulsion that registered forever. My Mama had basically undermined and demolished the statuesque and graceful personality she had always been for me. Suddenly, she had gone totally berserk, lost control, gone hysteric and reduced herself into a heap of ordinariness. I was so overwhelmed by her large eyes, her choking voice that I stepped back and left the house for the hills where my cousin lived. Something would unravel eventually, I said to myself. I had cycled up the hill in an inattentive manner.

In our house we did not follow any religion. Much to the aggravation of my grandfather and some others in the neighbourhood, it was clear that this household moved around with a flamboyant and dismissive attitude towards churches, synagogues and mosques. Maybe, it was not necessary on our part, but what came with it was the calm intellectuality associated with not getting swept away by religious edicts and fanaticism. In fact, it was natural as well to the community around us that religious affiliation was not a primary connection with the community around us. But what was not apparent was the undercurrent of suspicion and doubt about others that still persisted. So, there were some belligerent types who crossed back and forth over the bridge and caused substantial harm to our otherwise tolerant perspective as a community and as a nation.

This conspiratorial seclusion that I was subjected to finally got on my nerves and on the fifth day, I stormed back home.

It was then that I found out that Nika had died.

How? I did not know, then. Where was her body? Did someone kill her? Was she buried? How could she be buried so quickly? Why was I not told? Why was I spirited away and why was my Bo still not around and why had my mother betrayed me in such a way? Why had she broken the sense of confidentiality and closeness I had with her?

"We did not want you to be here, as she lay dead. Your Bo was not here and so I panicked, also. I did not want you around."

Nika was gone.

This was something so unbearable that my feet tottered, my mind went into a whirl of sadness and numbness. I sat down. I could not even begin to explain to myself how, within a short period of time, two deaths had left me totally bereft of the ability to seek reason in anything I did. Algebra? Equations? What for? It was like two flowers had suddenly wilted, keeled over, and the plants lay prostrate, withered in an instant. And I did not even see Nika. What was on her mind? Did she have an accident? Did she kill herself? Why did she not give me an inkling about what had happened? Why?

Certain traumas singe you to the bone. The bizarre way her death was smoothened out and even covered up, changed me forever. There was no solace to be found.

When I walked into her room, it seemed the floors had been washed impeccably, the bed linen was freshly done up and Lana Ester was actually cleaning her wardrobe.

She grabbed one of Nika's blouses and covered her mouth to suppress the scream that never came out of her when she saw me. The floors felt damp. The air was that of the outside, brought in by the opened windows. It was not the warm room my sister lived in. Its coldness was draining to the point that I stepped back and did not want to be there any longer. As I exited the morgue, I noticed at one corner of the wall, above her armoire—a congealed dark brown splatter on the wall. My mother had missed it. I knew it was not normal and never would be. From there on, Lana Ester no longer meant the same to me. She was somehow gone, as well. A complete erasure of the sound mother, the epitome of balance and intelligence, the sly humour that summarized the subtleties of understanding each other in the household. The bulwark, the rock cliff, the bow of the ship had been reduced to a wreck on the beach.

***

The War was coming to an end, soon. The Germans had sounded the retreat in El-Alamein. The Soviets were barrelling ahead to Berlin and Benito was under virtual house arrest. I realized that I was not going to be informed at that time about all that had transpired on the day before my forced expulsion to my relative's house up on the mountain. I would rather keep up with the news of the winding-down of the War. But can you imagine what had happened in such quick succession in my life? My sister went away like the splatter on the wall which needed to be mopped away with some bleach! Shaf had disappeared and his mother had been transformed into char in her own kitchen. And my Bo was in and out. Something that I could not absorb any longer. Sabzic was not my town anymore. I needed to get away.

It stood upright, on the left-hand side of the almirah in my sister's room. Like a sentinel was holding it up. The door had been left open inadvertently. I had never looked inside that almirah before. I saw the metallic sheen, like a sudden flash of light was coming from the opening in the middle. It was for sure not a piece of women's clothing. I opened the door slowly and saw what it was.

It said Remington Arms Company, Ilion, NY USA. 1890. The barrels had given it the sheen, that I had seen from the cracked open almirah. I looked closer and saw there were two hammers and the barrels were side by side. Although the wood was chipped here and there, it was majestically carved around the breech area and under the barrels, as well. This was the gun. The one that my grandfather had used to blast away at the fish some twenty years ago, and my Bo would have to jump into the river and scoop out the fish and toss them into the boat. I put my hand in to lift it out and Lana Ester came storming in again and pulled me away, shut the almirah. She stared at me, without saying a word.

"I need to know, what happened. If you do not tell me now, I will find out later. I will! I am thirteen. I have friends at school who have joined the partisans. This is not a family tragedy or something to be ashamed of. This is a disease from outside the walls of our house. From across the canal and past the bridge. It is coming from the borders of our country and beyond. It is brewing inside the soul of our nation, as well. My sister's death is a national shame. How did she die? Tell me!"

My short sermon must have shocked the hell out of her.

She stood in silence and stared at me with her head slightly tilted to the side. Her lower lip pouted a bit and after what seemed like an aching passage of time, a gentle smile emerged, her eyes glistened and her head nodded gently. She came closer and hugged me and then we went to the kitchen and she told me how she had to clean the floors, the bedsheets and even the walls.

My Bo came back the very next day. He held me in his arms. I felt a bit awkward, as my lanky bones jutted out into his robust frame. He was not crying. I suppose there were tears in my eyes. His forehead was sad. We held each other and my mum came by and sat down in the couch where Shaf would sit.

He left again after two days. I noticed the Remington was gone.

***

Political debates were not routine in our house. Ours was not a house that went into argumentative fits. The discussions were full of sighs, regrets, dismissive signals of the hand, references to the words of poets, and avoidance of certain issues. So, it was all left to me. A kind of "we are different" air, rose from our midst. I looked and stared at each speaker and while I kept quiet, I knew that it would eventually barrel through my soul, my blood, my veins in some order and remain forever. The silent stares in the house were often louder than the hollering my grandfather indulged in, in the plaza, with his flaring nostrils and an abundance of exaggerated emotions. Amidst all the sound of bombs falling, the sounds in the sky of warplanes, there was an extraordinary chemistry and compassion between my Mama and my Bo for the logic and raison d'être that they lived for and that sometimes seemed quite enthusing and yet puzzling for me.

They would begin to discuss a certain period of Goya and his paintings. Excitement soared in their eyes. And the grim sound of an explosion faraway would be ignored. If Shaf was around, he would join in, adding a level of randomness to the subdued energy level. He would even jump up, stand and then sit down as my Bo would ask him to settle down. My Bo smiled. Meanwhile, my Mama serenely reminded all that in that particular period of Goya, ugly faces became reflective of ugly times and ugly personages. A panoply of the grotesque. As an example, *The Pilgrimage of San Isidore*, she added, where a gathering of disfigured, disoriented, anguished hobgoblins trudge along towards a magic fountain—not sure of themselves. Like my grandfather's evil posse as they rushed over the bridge. And the clouds were dark, the mountains were darker and the faces were distorted with fury and hatred.

***

I went into Nika's room and walked around the bed. The window was slightly open and as the cold breeze probed the room in small bursts, I noticed that Shaf's diary had suddenly reappeared in her room. It was on her bedside table. It was wrapped in brown paper.

Lana Ester told me that Shaf had come back and given the diary to Nika, for safe keeping, pretty much right after I had dropped it off on the porch. I was possibly biking around the bridge, uselessly, when he dropped by. She teared up and told me what had happened when Shaf came. They sat together for an hour and she must have made those two feet high coffees she seemed to be making for him alone. And some biscuits. Nika and Shaf smiled and held hands. They seemed very happy, she said. But when Shaf was leaving, he told her that he was going to join my Bo somewhere. I was not sure—or at least I was not one hundred percent convinced—that Shaf would also join the fighters in the mountains. He would probably get all philosophical when the time came to fire back. Could I imagine him being part of an ambush? Never! But it was comforting to know that he had not gone trekking.

I was listening to Lana Ester recounting the evening that Shaf had come by to return the diary. I so desperately wanted to be there. I so wanted to deliver my prepared speech about my unpardonable ineptitude and sneakiness in not returning the diary.

"Did he say when he would be back?"

"No, he did not bring that up, at all. He just mentioned that he would be seeing your Bo, somewhere near Zurich."

Chapter Fourteen

Imagine if there was *one event* in your life that set a trench on fire inside your body, running through your veins, your seams, all the canals inside you. So chilling that it left an indelible scar on the rest of your existence. A searing groove cut in a straight line from that extraordinary event right up to every turning point in the rest of your life. And along the way, it influenced, pushed and corralled your thoughts and actions, even your beliefs, towards a similar direction. The event mysterious, mystical, intimidating or annoying, left questions unanswered, but was the centre of a quake that registered sharply then, and made you tremble even now. Did I have such an event in my life?

Let me explain. Imagine if you could explain all your hesitations, vicissitudes as well as your confident strides in any particular direction, as flowing from that one event? The event could have been inspirational or it could have been outright trauma, but it also had a satisfying mystical element to it, so much so that you longed to revisit it in your mind as often as possible.

As an example, I have read about a spiritual happening when a whole village trotted out once a year, in the middle of winter, to see the mystical blooming of a particular maroon flower inside a cavernous rock face and the withering of it within a week. No questions were asked, no answers were received. The event brought peace and calm to the hamlet. The silent trek up the mountain to see the flower bloom and die provided solace for each one. No words were exchanged, no sounds were heard. The silent procession headed up the hill. Meanwhile, tumult raged outside the valley, in the town further down below. Civil strife was rampant. Riots were happening. Houses were set on fire. But no one seemed to care in this silent caravan as it went up the mountain.

And I have heard of a situation in a neighbouring country, where there was the magical appearance of a goat on a hilltop at the same time, every year in a certain village. Then there were situations where the hands of a teacher in school wandered strangely over your limbs when you were only six years old. A cousin or a friend who disappeared in the middle of a family strife and nobody talked about it any longer. Pivotal events, no doubt.

But my single incident experience was something much simpler and yet crushing in what it conveyed. It was real and unforgettable. It was the sudden burst of shine that I saw coming out of the closet in my sister's bedroom, when the door was left open inadvertently. I kept revisiting it, although I did not have to, because that shine, that glint had already had a permanent impact on everything that I feared, dreaded, hated and yet imagined as some sort of an ominous symbol of things gone wrong. When I looked at the Remington, it stared back at me.

Years later I was being interviewed for my first job in a law firm and was asked to discuss how from childhood on, if there was there any single incident in world affairs that had

had a deep impact on me? This triggered the worst emotions in me. It was a way of testing the subconscious and a way of labelling my emotions and intelligence. As if a unifying set of events or values, dos and don'ts had continuously evolved and followed me around, after a single incident. I was uncomfortable and irritated. Like the hermits trekking up to a mountain top to view a flower or stare at a goat, what incident could prod me on? My life was not that of a peasant whose ideas were governed by the simplest miracles and bizarre happenings and I could not possibly describe that sudden shine that came out of the dark closet in my sister's room. It was my single incident that had brought together malevolence, defiance and ultimately restitution.

The interviewer kept prodding me.

"Was there a single moment that leaned on you heavily, to change the colours, to move away towards another ideal? Some irrational possibilities, even? Or, a fork in the road where you found yourself stimulated by something else and started to flirt with ideas that were attractive but simultaneously and intuitively absurd, utopian or even evil?"

It is as if he was already manipulating me to expose my subconscious! Lurid, I thought. It is aggravating when someone asks you what is your inspiration in life. There is no single fountainhead of inspiration! There is no single person, no body of thought, no formula, no events that could have been the only source of stimulus. There could be hundreds of incidents, several encounters with siblings, teachers and parents, scores of images of townsfolk getting irate following a funeral procession to a point where riot and mayhem became unforgettable, even memorable, where the mix of colours and the sudden incursions into the canvas of estranged colours, changed everything. And that could have all left a subliminal resonance. Is it not possible? But in my case, I did have that incident that was different and I could not explain it. Yet I felt it necessary to conceal it.

The interviewer was relentless. What was his intent? What was he really trying to establish? Was he looking for some suppressed deviance in me? From a single incident? Is that what was growingly being considered as a psychological assessment?

What if there were many mountains, many inspirations? What if there were many simple incidents that left a mark on your body and soul? Maybe a dog bite, maybe a car crash, maybe a boy who fell from a rooftop while flying a beautiful blue kite, maybe an assault, a nightmare and maybe a magnificent sunrise over a mountain that was just spectacular. In my case, there were many mountains and peaks and canvases. Actual mountains, actual towns, sunrises, dark moonlit nights and actual uncles whose hands wandered. And there was a plum tree in our house that bloomed every three years. And Lana Ester knew that, because every three years she made several bottles of plum jams with vanilla that lasted several years. "It's Botany!" said Shaf. "It is plant chemistry!"

But! The shine in my sister's closet was unforgettable.

***

My grandfather despite being only a prosecutor, had the reputation of being a hanging judge. He wanted the full force of the law applied on every infraction. He told everyone what to do, when to shut up. When incidents occurred, it was his interpretation that mattered. He tweaked his moustache like it was the final word after he delivered a terrifying discourse.

And then there was my father. He disliked confrontation. He simply walked away and did his own thing, far away from the grandfather's sphere of influence. He nodded his head and quietly snuck out, and when he had passed on to another room, a smile appeared on his lips. His way of saying, "Screw you! You old, sulking peevish man!" My Mama heard him even though he had not opened his mouth. And she smiled too, naughtily.

It was my father who gently planned an escapade from this situation and chose the medical profession as the planned strategy. He was soon out of the house and entrenched somewhere in the UK by the time he was twenty-two. He kept in touch with letters, explaining what he was up to. His letters were mailed to my mother's name and my mother would dutifully hand them over to me directly, if she felt alright about sharing it.

And there was my mother, herself. An expert on Magnetism who selected a life of planned repulsion or attraction to the world that was surrounding us. She had made a pact with my Bo, it seemed. Not to be discussed.

And the town we lived in was nestled in the middle of a deep valley, where a river snaked around, glistening brightly even at dusk, and disappearing into the distance. Towering mountains, greenish grey in summer, cast shadows over the valley; the town's churches, synagogues and mosques resisted all storms and floods for five hundred years or more and the citizens bickered amongst themselves to the sound of bells, horns, overpowering incense and rumours of invasions and the wailing call of the muezzins. And the lonely Romani hawker dragged his body across the bridge, mumbling "from dusk to dawn, dusk to dawn."

Despite all these sounds, aromas and the incredible scenery—overflowing greenery leaning on to flowing rivers and the sun bouncing off the curved stone bridge that was almost ornamental and distractive—there was that one distraction that sent shivers through me. I could not explain to the interviewer what it meant and how it had been pivotal to my life story.

Section Two

Shaf, the Remington
and the Principia

Chapter Fifteen

Today, December 1, 1943, Joseph Stalin met Winston Churchill and Franklin Roosevelt. The meeting was held in Teheran, in the Soviet Embassy. A meeting to make very clear to the whole world as to who was on whose side. To dispel doubts, in the minds of average citizens, that there was virtue and higher morality in the souls of most nations. These moral nations would not tolerate doctrines that believed in racial superiority and the extermination of people for their race or religion. This was not a meeting about battle tactics or technology. Or, what the bore of a standard issue pistol should be so that the magazines, barrels and the bullets could be billeted out for manufacturing in any allied country. It was, however, billed as a meeting of political unity, about "opening a second front." And the Normandy invasion project, code-named *Overlord*, was thereby initiated. But, as I would have told Ben, I was not going to be fooled. Morality is not even skin deep. It is like the thick cream that sits on top of boiled milk: Fat and light. Easily removed and tossed into the sink.

Because until then, both Churchill and Roosevelt were playing a wait-and-see game to ascertain if the Soviets could handle the Nazis on their own. Depending on who would prevail, they would negotiate with the winner. Unfortunately for them, the Red Army prevailed and Churchill and Roosevelt had to come to the meeting. Photo-smiles were dished out for the world to see. The stilettos were deftly concealed in their winter coats. Churchill wore an oversized one and resembled very much a neckless toad, breathing through his gills and forcing air into his lungs. Roosevelt was having difficulty moving around and Stalin sat upright, wary and looking around.

December 1 was my birthday, as well. I realized that late in the afternoon because I felt a discreet longing for the taste of *Ćufte* and *pilav*, which my mother made on that date. Especially when I put my mouth to the hard sausage distributed to our platoon, which had to be twisted into my mouth with partisan fervour—but it had turned out to be sweet, sour and phlegmy. Something had fermented. So, I tossed it away and sat down on a plank in the trench, crossed my legs like the Teheran trio, stared into the trench wall, a good three feet away from my face, and scribbled some notes. I waited to hear some crackle from the radio.

"Would you ever hold a gun?" he asked, his eyebrows raised sincerely.

Ben, the boy I had been coaching in Algebra for two years, asked onerous questions. For a second, I thought he was asking me if I was physically capable of holding one, and then I realized he was actually asking if I believed in using one. He was intense, this kid. He saw my hesitation and continued.

"Could you kill someone, because of his ideas?"

I was just about to say, Yes! I could! But that would be thoughtless.

"And what would killing do to that someone, if he had written down his ideas in a diary that was hidden away and discovered years later?" Now, he was being a child. He persisted in probing me.

"True!" I said. "If ideas could be written down or even spread by word of mouth, then it would be futile to kill an individual for his opinions and ideas."

Ben, with his thirteen years of wisdom, saw no purpose in killing off individuals.

But, did he understand why nations invaded other nations?

Did he understand what wars were all about? Did he understand that memories of defeat and humiliation persist in the soul of nations?

Did he understand occupation? Did he understand hatred, suspicion, intolerance? Did he also understand that wars were not always about egotistical leaders, but could be crafty grand plans hatched by a handful of extraordinarily wealthy entities, be they in one nation or many, to dominate others by any means?

Did he understand that people who had lived and shared each others' culture, languages, could turn suspicion into an animus of hatred that mushroomed into seething anger and eventually built up into an orgy of rioting, lynching, arson and finally invasions?

This boy could get on my nerves with his questions. His Bo should have answered all these questions, is it not true? And did he understand that religion could be a real whore! Yes, a whore! Who in a fit of frenzy and contempt could lift her skirt up and piss on the cobblestones in the plaza and on the adjoining bed of flowers, maroon, violet, pink—so much so that the sounds of the torrent would resonate and make heads turn—and the flow of the piss would destroy every-thing that ever grew on that soil? Turn the flowers to straw. And the soil to ashes. And sometimes religion would go into a meditative daze and sermonize on peace, happiness and forgiveness and the whore would weep. Maybe that is not a great analogy, but it is the way I feel. That religion is pretty, peaceful, remedial—until it reaches the end of its seductive appeal and unleashes terror and destruction.

Because that is what had happened in our country. Bridges were built; canals were designed; roads were paved; churches, mosques and synagogues were erected to allow people a consensus on their beliefs, their shelters for intro-spection. When introspection was undermined, the cit-izens became unruly. They began to run to the bridges, the plazas and the streets to demonize each other. The iconic towers of acceptance and tolerance were turned into rubble. Despair and separation took over. Did Ben understand that armies marched to seize ports so that they could control seaways? Did he understand that war was an exercise in overwhelming other communities, of exercising superiority, of massacres, when required? War was quite a package, I would say. Well-arranged, organized and invigorating—that contained all the elements of personal anger, animos-ity, religious and nationalist arrogance and megalomaniac notions of control.

I do understand the concerns of Ben. That a gun cannot kill an idea. Killing is purely a one-to-one affair. Meaning that I shoot you when you are just about to shoot me. Or, I shoot you—knowing fully well that you are unarmed. Pure malice is often a requirement that the gun demands of you.

***

Meanwhile, as I looked out over the edge of the trench and into the horizon and in the far distance on the dusty road ahead, I could imagine the Wehrmacht was approaching, while I sat cross-legged. They have field guns, mortars, flame throwers, tanks and air support. That army has the notion that invasion and occupation is necessary. On the other hand, we feel that we must stay in our trenches and fire back. Or, we must withdraw, split up into small groups and harass the invading force from the flanks. Till we can pick them off, one by one, from the hilltops. I am learning all this. This is not a question of using a gun. It's a question of using what's up here, in the head. This Ben bugs me with that single question, he asked. It bounced around inside my head, like a bagatelle round.

Let me explain something. If I say something like…all men are basically good, it means simultaneously, that all men could be basically bad. Because as there exist good men, there exists bad men. Good exists because there is bad. Whatever exists is actually a recognition of what does not. So, he needs to also understand that there is death only because life exists.

It is a question of belief, my friend! Beliefs and ideas keep us alive. And when we work hard to transform those beliefs into a flow of ideas, it allows people to embrace these ideas—for a while, at least. If death intervenes, there is another life that steps in.

But not everything exists because of its antithesis. Intervention makes things change. Like the flow of ideas! It is like having a cup of tea. You have to pour it into a cup, right? So, you need a spout. Because, otherwise you would be making a mess if there was no spout on the kettle. Even the lip on the spout is designed to ensure that the flow can be controlled by adjusting the angle of the tilt. The flow. The spout channels the tea with extraordinary precision into the mug or the cup. I am convinced that if all ideas could flow out of a central reservoir at a steady pace and then be controlled back when it gets too overwhelming, that would provide peace of mind and tranquility to the human race. Ideas can live. However, you cannot let things overflow. I am not crazy. I am not a madman. I know the flow of ideas must be controlled.

And he is asking, could I use *this* device! Does he have a bullet in his hand? What audacity this boy has!

That finely shaped conical cylinder, which projects a metal nose, spiralling through the air, penetrating the outer boundaries of a person's body, drills through his flesh, bones and organs and exits from another point in his body—can this kill the idea, inside that body? I did not think so either. But, on the other hand, was there ever an occasion where a refined debate, arranged auspiciously between two arguing nations, in a grand arena, resulted in a victory for one idea and defeat for the other—and the two parties would shake hands and hug—while the victorious party would take over the land of the other, wipe out its language and culture and even its food habits, its music and its historians and archivists and the members of the defeated camp would submit like lambs to this loss as a logical outcome of a fair debate?

To resolve everything that engulfs me in the world of Physics, Mathematics, Philosophy and the pesky nuances of History where humans repeat the mistakes of the past, and yet enthusiastically carry on to repeat them again and again, could I ask myself this same question? Could intervention—the act of killing—be a salve, an analgesic, or even a temporary anodyne?

Here I am with boots and a heavy camouflage jacket on, a 9mm pistol on my belt, as I grip an M91 Carcano pointed at the road, several hundred metres below. The sour smell of sweat permeates through this olive-coloured jacket, as I take up a prone position in a trench, along the northernmost ridges of what remains the country whose citizenship I hold. As I crouch and start losing focus on the road, I think of Ben, because he is still alive somewhere. Asking questions; but his sister is not and neither is my mother, nor my father.

My father's death in the United States had not really shocked me. He could have died of tuberculosis in a sanatorium in Finland and it would not have made any difference to me. I was too young to know what a father could be. The sound of rockets launched some distance away makes me aware of the present, but I do not wish to lose my train of thought.

The fact that he had been run over by a train while trying to rescue a child was distressing and something I did not want to think of and yet, it was something I frequently reframed in my mind. We were waiting for him to arrange our trip over. The United States was stepping into a new period of building infrastructure then. Roads, highways, canals, bridges, airports creating networks. I hear more gunfire. The staccato sounds of a Bren spitting away further down below in the bushes, just before the road curves around the next mountain slope. The United States is just down the road.

The networks spread commerce in the US. Networks that infuse life into what is an ancient predicament where local production saturates local needs but cannot grow, because the cost of transportation is forbidding. Roadways and bridges make the market bigger and the producers, more dynamic. It provides jobs. It creates collaboration between the private and the public. It builds wealth, does it not? The firing is more intermittent. It does not sound like our people. But who are they? And the Germans still have not reached that part of the country. I pick up my telescope and look on the edges of the next valley. I do not see any movement. I hear the radio crackle.

The Sears Roebuck company started out as a watch-making outfit. As soon as the highways and railroads started being built up, Sears became a mail-order catalogue company! Now, is that not a groundbreaking transformation? What a leap of the innovative bourgeois mind! My father was a player in that grand experiment of rapid industrialization out of the expansion of the transportation network. He spoke one among many alien languages spoken along the railway lines. His death was a milestone for our family. The first, that I knew of anyway. I had not known death before. Then the War came and in quick succession my mother and my sweetheart were erased. Did I understand these three deaths? Was I capable of understanding loss? Of course, I did! And when Nika was taken away, do you think I suffered in silence?

The gunfire had almost stopped. Were they allies or were they those who could not make up their minds about us?

When she was gone, I went to the stone bridge and stared down into the flow, until the flow came closer and closer to my eyes, like I could touch it, put my hands in it. Without any hesitation, I gracefully dove into the river from the bridge. It was to wash myself, feel the stampeding current while the trout and the loose rocks tore into my face; and then I stopped crying under the water. Because I did not want anyone to hear my screams. Least of all Ben. The water muffled my cries and my tears became irrelevant, and after I had swum almost a mile downstream, swallowing the river, I slowly moved to the bank and sat down at the Strand. And I remained sitting at a bench, for a few hours, until the river had nearly dried from my body. It was a logical thing to do, while I shivered. People may have thought I was crazy! This is not lunacy! It is a restoration of balance. I was not going to go home, lie down on a cot till my heart stopped. I slept on the bench, all night. There was no home.

Ben! I must tell you something. When I found out what had happened, my heart went into an unpredictable rhythm and everything inside me felt stripped and ripped apart. Shredded. And I had nowhere to go and my inside started falling out like debris. There was nothing I could do.

Your sister was a wave of maroon across a trembling moonlit night. A splash across the sky, hard to decipher, but her signature was evident, as I looked up. When morning came, the rays of blue and maroon dissolved, and she bounced around and raced across the field, where the yellow shivered, as the winds swept through the fields in waves. She was the wave, the break from everything that I had ever known.

You are a perceptive genius. You are surrounded by well-meaning parents who have trained you in the most subtle manner to observe and absorb, rather than barge into an argument, pointlessly. You ask questions only if you are confounded. You are not repetitive and you often seem bored, which really instigates my curiosity. There is something about you that I find quite mysterious. I love you. Yet people think I am a lunatic! They will call you one, soon. I am not upset by your questions.

Nika was a minuscule element in the fabric of the nation. A thread, that had to drift away out into the future, and not get caught in the wars that surrounded her. She was open and direct. Ben, on the other hand, was reserved—looking for answers to questions that had not yet been asked. He did not ask about wars and coups or assassinations. He asked about how and where rights and obligations—of people, nations and governments—converged. He asked about the future state. He asked about the establishment of laws and not about violations of it. She had to pay the price.

The five-hundred-year history of conflicts, wars, invasions and sagacious attempts at constructing new nations, whether free of prejudice or defined by religious nationalism, went back and forth and got easily mangled up in the politics of regional powers. Some of these were the dreams and attempts of Kings to construct empires that they thought would last forever. Behind it all was the insane pursuit of the hypotheses that power and its perpetuation is paramount. Newton's Principia had framed the mathematical basis of philosophy and in turn laid the basis for every grand exercise in society. Logic and discreet interconnections laid the basis of both evil and good ideas. Was that accurate?

Brother and sister were possibly way ahead of their time, in their own ways.

I did not hear the sound of tanks that night, rolling down the road, a mile away, with their crackling sound, engines coughing and wheezing, with the turrets bobbing up and down, appearing and disappearing between the fir trees.

The monster in Rome or in Berlin had been almost defeated but they had left behind recalcitrant and defeated souls who could never reconcile themselves. Whether you were

Stjepan or Ivan, you would not want to live under a Goran or a Zoran. That wound would surface. Meanwhile, Amir and Tarik, you ask?

***

These notes that I write in my diary, which Ben had temporary control over for a while, are my testament; and I would like Ben to steal it again, some day. And perhaps he will then understand how tormenting it is to be continuously confounded by the relationship between matter, force, gravity, inertia at the atomic level, and the unexplainable behaviour between people, governments, organizations and nations at the ground level. They are under constant force constraints. But human actions are not conforming to any atomic or molecular behaviour! Why? And yet, we have atoms zipping in and out of structures and orbits within our bodies and brains. Why then is there this discrepancy? Why is it that the Physics and Chemistry we learn in colleges is not applicable to the behaviours of humans that we encounter? Why in the psychology of individuals and the psychosis of nations are atomic interaction and forces not in play? Is hysteria, hatred and madness not atomically governed? Why do the charges on an electron, which are supposed to be consistent, not control our psychosis?

I have to call it a closure now. I hear chatter on the radio and I can hear Ben's Bo asking us to move out of the trenches immediately and move into the forest. The word is that Panzer movement had been found by our trackers. They could be on us, any moment. Move, he repeated! And I was busy plotting our withdrawal, using a compass on a weary map.

Like Archimedes I could have said, "Do not disturb my circles." But I packed up and started moving.

Chapter Sixteen

When I confounded Ben with my scant but practical knowledge of quantum theory—and about how it could come into conflict with the world of Newton—he seemed a bit disturbed and even angry. Naturally. Because, he had just come to know that the first and second laws of Newton were nearly God-given. Not retractable. Then I brought up quantum theory! He was convinced that scientists were living in a bubble. "Cut off from reality!" as he said.

I tried to explain that reality was relative and measurable, especially when large and observable, but when it came to very small particles, matter, force and energy did not behave in a similar manner. There was an element of probability introduced and matter or waves did not obey Newtonian physics. For example, large observable stuff like a horseman travelling from point A to point B on the Alps, was real—but it was also a question of observing the horseman, from a point C or point D, and recording his move from point A to B. But I also went on to say that photons bashing against each other or against a photo plate was also travel, but it was travel that left a trace, that was often quite different. It provided a record and that much of reality was observation and it was the act of observation and recording that was fundamental. Not the result. I did not think I was purposely putting on an act or baffling him. But he was offended. My main intent was to take him on to the concept of ideas travelling and having the same impact as force on an object. In other words, I wanted him to know or understand that like quantum mechanics, ideas do not have the same impact on the opinion of people. That people have a built-in psychosis and truth or reality cannot prevail on everyone in the same way. But what is that built-in psychosis?

"Does Shaf not seem a bit distracted?" whispered Lana Ester to the Bo.

"No! Actually he climbs on top of a mountain in a frenzy and does not know how to come down. It's ok!" Ben's father asserted casually. I could overhear their whispering in the next room.

I suspected that they thought that I was going off. But they did not want to discuss it with me. My mother felt so, as well. She thought I had reached some elevated level of irrationality. And the next step would require me to be treated or confined. She was worried. Ben's Mum, the divine Mrs. Ester, was different. She was more reflective and adored me, otherwise she would not make those special two-feet-high coffee pours, and fantastic cakes. She felt that I was not happy and needed frequent interactions beyond Ben, and she shared that with Nika. But Nika knew that being disturbed is not bad and it is actually good for me. It made me productive! That is what she relayed to me with a shy smile.

"When you think out loud, you are simultaneously making up things, which you had not thought of! Isn't it?" She was like a prober. She opened up so many pathways.

But it was on their faces. Also, about my mother! How could I have nothing to say about my mother's murder, any longer? We all knew who did it. Was I incapable of sorrow or revenge? That was what they felt. Or, maybe that is what I felt, they felt. Did I live only on theories?

I never saw the family thereon for a long time. I could not see Mrs. Ester anymore. Except I met Ben's father in Zurich. In the early spring of 1943. He had asked me to join him there for an important meeting.

The month of this entry is not clear, as my diary was not from the current year. By February 2, 1943, the Sixth German Army surrendered in Stalingrad. Ninety-one thousand soldiers and twenty-four generals included. It was the first and only real defeat of a large German offensive. However, the battles in the Atlantic, the sinking of U-boats and the breaking of the German code received far greater news coverage.

I was beginning to sense a bit of tension within our platoon. While the enemy was clear on our gunsights, we would also be looking sideways at our trench mates. Now, why was that?

All three Abrahamic faiths believe in one God. Elohim, Abba or Allah. But why is there not one source book of knowledge? From which all three can write their religious edicts? Of course, not possible! Islam is much younger. How impudent of me! But they all have an underlying mission to maintain and preserve their rule by an omnipotent state in their own ways, with their own systems and their own rules. An ordered hierarchical sense of conduct, governed by an awe-inspiring state. When something catastrophic happens, like an assassination, a crop failure, a famine, a series of bank failures, a plague or an impudent horse-riding barbarian arrives from over the mountains primarily to expand his looting and plundering career, then the state does not encourage you to say prayers. The state must swing into action, using the apparatus of the state, mobilizing its forces. Also, the state must be immunized, walled off from such calamities. Preserved and protected for the future. The state is immutable. Religion is put away in the cellar, on hold. The state is a constitutionalized structure of beliefs, ideals and a deft way to preserve the status quo, for whichever clan is in power.

However—and I emphasize HOWEVER—each religion felt they were better than the others in maintaining the state. For example, even such a defunct religious sect like the Gnostics who walked around with royal airs, high and mighty, based on personal experience as the basis of their superior access to secret knowledge and undermined the spread of scientific knowledge, erected a sense of the state. Magic and deep secrets combined to confound everyone. Divinity was a must to escape from this confinement on earth. Survival was only possible if all people acquired knowledge in controlled doses. We were actually divine souls trapped in our bodies and to be released we must acquire knowledge at an even pace. Thus, religion stayed alive in the cellars.

And there were the Byzantines, the Latinos, the Greeks, the Venetians and even the Mongols—all came by to try out their luck at occupation and defining the state. The Ottomans had the longest run of success. What was their state secret?

***

The Ottomans injected a higher level of governance through their invention of personal law, which was called a *millet*. So, it did not matter what confessional community you belonged to, you could go to an independent court and resolve issues and get a ruling under your own laws. So, whether you are aligned to the Sharia, the Canon or the Halakha, you could seek a separate ruling and everyone was given a triangulated portion of the pie to chew on. What it did was to preserve the oven where everything was baked and then apportion the pie to all parties. The oven was the state. It was invisible, not subject to change. It was controlled by the majority millet. The other millets lived in their own quarters, satisfied that they were rulers of their own destiny. The fact that the state itself may need to be overhauled or overthrown, was not contested. Integration by separation was what some cynics would say. Clever.

My mother made toast on an ill-functioning toaster. And then would ask me to spread the butter evenly. Even if the toast was burnt to carbon dust. I once pointed out to her that there was an element of a dysfunctional state here and she looked up at me, for a few seconds and then nodded her head gently, with cynicism prancing around her cheeks, as her head nodded from side to side in derision. Then she provided a compromise solution, with a gentle smile. Just like a priest would.

"Next time please scrape it off and then butter it. It may not be too bad. You have a right to do that, believe me!"

"But Ma, the burnt smell lingers!"

It is the way the toaster is built and the fact that you have to stand there and watch it. No controls. It is a fancy art deco Scandinavian product, all chrome—which my mother bought from a Romani in Prague. It is an attractive and ornamental piece on our little dinner wagon, in the dining room. But it was perfectly useless. I would not tell her that, because she would be hurt. Nothing was brighter than the toaster in our house. Also, she would say that I was being precocious. Her aesthetic was to be left alone! In the end the toaster was preserved, until our house itself got burnt down. The toaster remained a symbol of my childhood. It did not work, but if we stood there next to it and unplugged it, it was okay! The right to unplug as necessary was upheld as autonomy.

The state settles issues. In such situations, intelligent Machiavellians and semi-enlightened Dukes, Barons, Vazirs or a colloque of interested religious parties takes on the challenge of defining and building a state that accommodates the essence of all spiritual beliefs, including the failures to explain many phenomena and then presents a condescending and paternalistic decision as to how the state must settle differences. Each group with its own areas of operation. Separate but integrated! To preserve the state. To salvage the dignity of the toaster. That is why the millet system, while secular in appearance, laid the basis of the state being in the hands of the larger millet! The Ottomans were far ahead of Venice or Constantinople in that sense.

***

I want to be left alone when I kneel down to my God. I do not want to be part of a congregation, a huge collection of people dipping in a river full of piss and feces and hugging and caressing each other. I do not want to be a part of an order that sways and mumbles collectively, that it is getting rid of Satan in our midst and then dips into a poison chalice and commits collective suicide. And I do not want to be part of an

143

empire that erases history by making a mosque into a church or a synagogue into a mosque—and announce—"Nothing happened here, as of today!" And then the plastering is done and then the re-plastering. And then a century later, when the silica and the calcium trickle down and fall as dust on travellers and worshippers, the layers appear underneath—it becomes an archaeological finding! And as a people we feel sanctified, believed-in and acknowledged for our long-drawn-out sacrifices in building the state. Did we really build a state that was invincible?

Chapter Seventeen

I came back from the mountains—after a series of training sessions. In the late evening, I managed to slip into the area that was our home. The ruins had not been cleared. There was no one to do that work. There was no one to claim the property either. I walked onto the floor that was my bedroom. I found some books lying around on a low metal shelf that had survived the arson attack. I retrieved some of them that were not destroyed. Among them a copy of *The Principia*. Published in 1860.

I could not bury my Mum. She had to be scraped off the porch, where she lay down with a shovel in her hand. A melting metal table had fallen on her, as one of the legs had dissolved first. There was some irony in that Newton survived and proved that books and documents have a greater chance of survival than those who had attempted to preserve them. Outside on the porch, rainwater had combined with the ashes to form lye. Which I knew was like soap water. Like bleach, it clarifies everything. The blue and white mosaic on the floor of the porch was clear and clean. Like someone had polished it. I had never seen it so obviously majestic and glorious. Even Byzantine colours are often tedious or excessively lurid. But this blue smiled at you. I put the books in my rucksack and moved on.

***

In these past few days, as the War seems to be coming to an end, Dresden has been chosen to be pulverized to dust—like a very convincing, stentorian voice coming from the clouds. The Allies were telling the Germans, "Surrender! Motherfuckers! Sooner, or else…."

At one time, Dresden was known as the Florence of the Elbe. And unlike Berlin, Linz, Munich or Nuremberg, it was not really central to the war plans and strategies of the Fuehrer as he strutted around, screamed and stomped in his bunkers, either in the Wolfsschanze or Berghof. In fact, Adolph had abandoned all his forces and moved them to defend Berlin at any cost. If the Soviets wanted, they could roll into Dresden, without a bullet being fired at them. Ben would understand all this. He was a thoughtful boy, who understood reason!

In any case, between the Partisans, the Soviet Army and the Allies, who were mainly Americans, the British (with their thousands of colonial soldiers, engineers, doctors and paramedics), some Canadians, some Dutch, (the French—except for the Free French, led by De Gaulle—lost it early on and hid behind a line named Maginot, collaborating with the Axis and were soon occupied) and China in the east—and a whole host of nations across Asia and Africa had wreaked havoc on Adolphus' formidable Wehrmacht and so had the Chinese on the Japanese. As was quite well known, there was nothing in Dresden, militarily, to be attacked or destroyed. The destruction, though, turned out to be something that would rarely be discussed.

146

In Sabzic, a lone man stood by, on May 15, 1945, in an alley at five in the evening, behind a pillar. He was slightly stooped, as he looked around the corner with some stealth. The sun was dipping low over the tree line. He wore a robe with a hood and while he did not look like a monk, he did seem like he belonged to the type of disquieting religious cults that huddle around small fires and murmur ambiguous incantations to an absent Delphic leader. But he was eerie and of that, there was no doubt. He had a big bag, lying on the base of a marble pillar, next to him. The bag was zipped closed. He kept looking towards the town on the north side and then looked back at the bag next to him. His creepy tension was transported to the pigeons on the ledge of the city's domed municipal hall, and they made short fluttering movements, exchanging places and hopping erratically over each other.

On this day the radio said several hundred Lancaster bombers had continued carpet bombing Dresden. There were hardly any military targets there, but that had never been a matter of concern when you were fighting under a banner of liberation. The German air defences were nothing to speak of. The radio said 1400 tons of British bombs had careened off the bomb bays and sloped down the predicted path starting out, I suppose at zero vertical velocity and let's say 300 miles per hour (134 metres/sec) as horizontal velocity—that is the plane's average horizontal velocity. The vertical velocity components of the bomb, being Vo and Yo, which are both equal to zero at the time of release, the bombardier had a stupidly easy job here, flying at 1 mile (1609 metres) above the ground. So, solving for Y, in the equation $y=at^2$, where $a=9.8m/sec^2$, the acceleration due to gravity, we find t=18secs. So, 18 seconds before flying over the intended target, the bomber could unleash mayhem down below. As I had explained some time ago to Ben, precision is critical. The quest for precision is intrinsic to hitting targets accurately and justly, and that applied to ideals, as well. Without precise details about the present, it is impossible to aggregate and predict the future turn of events. The arc of the future. Without precision, any engagement would yield unpredictable results. But! One of the pitfalls of paying excessive importance to details, and the Germans easily succumb to details, is that you would not always be capable of deciphering the deviousness in the mind of a crazed military planner, whether of Allied or of Axis persuasion.

I continued my lessons with Ben, even when he was absent.

"If your intent is to *carpet bomb* a city, you do not have to calculate the horizontal distance from the target or the time of release. Is it not so? You just close your eyes and keep opening the release mechanism; you might as well howl, laugh, yawn, cheer and jeer at the Nazis below as you shriek and scream and deliver justice as the bomb rolls away! Right? There are no eighteen seconds required. Such was the bombing plan for Dresden."

Absent Ben was not pleased. In fact, he was quite disturbed by my cynical display of mirth in relation to the mayhem and murder that was happening on earth—and particularly as part of my attempts to explain the equations of motion of falling objects. I looked at him with some amusement. He did not look back at me. The trench wall looked back, perplexed. I was sounding cocky and as some would say quite insane! But I am not and as you will see I have had to fight this accusation continuously.

"But, why are you talking about carpet bombing? It is so cruel and criminal!" he said.

I told you, Ben is so sincere that it numbs me.

"Ah! Look at this way..." I continue.

I have not seen Ben in many months now, but I keep talking to him still as his coach and tutor. I am marching around the room, where I taught him. At times, Nika moves the curtain and is watching me. Or, I am marching around the room, where I take shelter in the middle of the town.

"...the bomber does not require any calculation if there are instructions to carpet bomb! You just pull the hatch open for a certain number of seconds, and the bombs land on canals, then houses, then bridges, then museums, then churches, then again on houses, then schools, then stadiums, then museums, then schools, then houses and then on the huge architectural masterpieces in marble that are waiting to be kissed gently, before they explode into a thousand fragments of marble, plaster, bolts, nuts, wood and steel support beams, and a motherlode of human flesh, blood, bones and corpuscles rise up like a fountain, as they sail through the air and land on some still existing rooftops, or the grey cobblestone plazas, below. There is no democracy, no secular thought processes involved in this act carried out every few seconds, as opposed to the 18-second precision plan, before one is over the target."

I take a break from this thespian display that I had gotten into, not realizing that my rising volume had attracted some kids in the trench who were staring at me. I told them the following, straight to their faces.

"And Ben would still not agree with me." They immediately looked away. Not knowing what to say.

"And for sure, the incendiary bombs were particularly effective. The whole city was in flames!" Every single, tempered, strengthened, glass window in the city's buildings and churches had been blown out. The shattered glass had come down like piercing missiles at the huddles of humanity, that had taken shelter in the churches, after their houses had been flattened.

Ben would not be amused by my attempt at being so dramatic about teaching him the equations of velocity and acceleration, with such morbid examples.

But what I never had a chance to tell him, is that in reality it did happen and several hundred American planes came by, after the RAF had left, and took out the railway stations, bridges, transportation hubs and killed off several thousand more civilians in wave after wave of sorties. At one mile above the ground and flying at 300mph, with navigators in support of pilots and bombers, they had delivered a flattened and smoldering city. I later found out that the Americans came by again and again and dropped another 2,800 tons on Dresden. The Allies say they were facilitating the Soviets on the ground. Now, this is war and no one really is going to figure out what happened when the history books are compiled.

The hooded monk-like figure tightens the rope belt around his hip and starts to open the big black bag that was lying at the base of the pillar. I knew that bag very well. There are hardly any people in the plaza. If there are any, they are cowering as the lamps are flickering on the Strand and the fountains have very little water dribbling out of them. Abruptly, the monk-like figure straightens up and looks straight at the archway on the southern side of the plaza.

A coach has appeared and the horses are trotting slowly towards the corner where it will take a turn towards the outskirts of the city. At this point the bag has been fully opened and the monk-like figure assumes a prone position near the bag. He is waiting for a signal.

The first pictures of the Baroque splendour that Dresden was famous for, often referred to with some degree of smugness as the Centre of European civilization, have started to appear in a trickle of newspapers that are still being hawked at the plaza. Unrecognizable, as some say. Opera Houses flattened to the ground, as if they were never constructed. There are pictures of marble towers occasionally sticking out in the coarsened landscape, the corner supports of large buildings, museums or churches, with mangled iron beams holding them up somehow. The clouds are like greying minstrels blowing mouthfuls of themselves at each other. Is this possible? Then there is the circular, welded steel frame that survived while the domes themselves got blown into the insides of the building. There are people trying to look for bodies of their relatives, who lie in the streets, eyes opened and staring out, as if there was no oxygen left in the air and their hearts had simply stopped halfway through taking a breath.

The hooded man has now brought his bag near to the corner of the street, where he knows the phaeton would turn. That is the point at which it slows down. The phaeton comes closer to the corner and the horse hooves make a uniform clip-clop sound on the cobbled road. The sun is on its way down, hovering a bit, until it disappears abruptly. There is almost no one visible in the square, where normally hundreds of people mill around. Except there are some Romanis sitting on the parapets, near the Strand. A man in a leather jacket, standing near the fountain unnoticed until now—only a hundred yards away—raises his hand and the hooded man rushes to the corner, lifts out a huge double barrel gun from inside the bag and walks over to the phaeton as it slows down. He points the gun at the coachman, who simply drops his reins, jumps out and bolts towards the Strand. The horses slow down and the gun is heard twice across the plaza and in the entire central square. Pigeons fly off in one huge cloud of fluttering wings from the top of the dome, which was once a Byzantine church. The body of the prosecutor rolls out from the open door, upside down, and his face stares from the foot-stand, his mouth open, his tongue hanging out, as he looks up at his deliverer.

"You bastard...for all that I did..." and he starts to chortle.

The man reloads carefully and finishes him off with considerable composure.

"You do not deserve to live one more day, Sir!"

He then takes the Remington back to the big bag, places it carefully and zips it up. The sound of the zipping is pronounced and augmented by the pigeons who flutter off again. The two horses, temporarily startled, recover to bring the phaeton to the side of the pavement and the prosecutor's head bounces a bit on the cobblestones. Then the horses get spooked somehow, and start to gallop and, the head bouncing on the cobblestones, start all over again, and the carriage is seen moving away till it reaches the end of the plaza and the horses execute a smart turn to stop under a lamp, where the prosecutor often stopped to pick up a newspaper. His body rolls out and settles on the drain, next to the pavement. *Dans le caniveau.* The Serf walks away quietly, carrying the bag on his shoulder. Long shadows form behind him. The diminutive and lifeless voice of the Romani at the Strand is heard, "from dusk to dawn, from dusk to dawn."

***

And yes, I did want to teach Da Vinci and Michelangelo as well as Newton, perhaps, together. However, I got kicked out of college, just for that. To put it succinctly, Da Vinci understood proportionality and science in art. Lighting and anatomy governed his works. Michelangelo was subsumed by emotional disturbances and tension represented by either airborne men in high-domed azure skies or earthbound men, grimacing in search of identity. What I wanted to teach and emphasize was what lay somewhere in between. The intersection of the laws of motion with the passage of ideas. But passion and obsession, dear Ben, could lead to neurosis.

Chapter Eighteen

Ben's Bo went by several names. Sometimes, as Dr. Pyotr. A chilling name for an extremely gentle and affable man. At other times he was Giovanni, the fluent Italian speaker who loved making coffee in the trenches from aluminum cans. And sometimes simply as Stepan. An enigmatic character. From reputedly being a doctor, he now operates in the mountains.

He is a naturally soft-spoken person; he never grabs the stage or attempts to command it. Ben did not talk about him, nor did his Mama or Nika. How could they? They were his own, and such an intimate experience for them. Not a hero, but a presence. They all joked with him and Nika even when she was just past twenty, would climb up on his lap and curl up. They were understandably happy and sad when he appeared and then disappeared. But they knew, they knew—I tell you—that he was an *inaudible* hero. The one that spoke with his eyes.

And as far as fathers go, mine got sliced up on a rail line. I had to write that in.

Bo was reputed to have studied medicine in England. In London to be specific. He was in his forties when I first met him.

"Would you like to coach my son? He needs help with his Algebra and History. I think you can do it. You can come over twice a week. He is easily distracted and likes to ask a lot of questions, in order to avoid homework. The headmaster in his school has advised me and his Mama that he needs help."

"Sure, I could. It is not too far from my house. I will take my bike and could be there in half an hour."

He said he would start paying right away and gave me an advance immediately.

And then in the days to come, he asked me with a sparkle in his eyes, about the debate around Neils Bohr.

We were both attending an information session about Adolphus' tanks, just a bit further up from Sabzic, in a small hamlet next to the banks of the river. He had asked me to come along. He had that sparkle in his eyes when he talked me into coming for the meeting. Here the mountain began to emerge, straight from the rocky banks of the river; the valleys narrowed down and gradually became gulleys and there were no roadways as such. There were creases around his eyes as well, as they narrowed, as he questioned me. Horses were the best mode of transport. What horses could do, the tanks could not. So the tanks invariably got stuck and became prime targets for ambush. The idea was to draw the tanks into the valleys and away from the high roads and closer to the gulleys. Then they either got immobilized or rolled over and gravity took over. I really did not get a chance to explain what I had understood about the big debate between Albert Einstein and Neils Bohr. It was in 1927 that these debates had started and I was barely seven years old then. But, by the time the War had started and I was around nineteen, I had acquired a popular understanding of quantum mechanics and entanglement and with that I was able to inform Dr. Pyotr, and as well, confuse the hell out of young Ben.

The Doctor had come by boat and had tied it down to the trunk of a tree with a rope. The knot came off and the boat started drifting. I saw him running after it, wading in and bringing the boat back. I was sitting at the back of the group, leaning against a tree, and he came and joined me with his clothes all wet. He was rugged as hell. He saw in my satchel, a physics textbook, his eyes narrowed and he asked me with a smile, "So who is right—Einstein or Bohr?" A pensive man with a large forehead. And thinning hair. He spoke softly and rarely raised his voice. Never showed any emotions. You would not know if he was happy or sad. He listened, smiled sometimes, and for the most part, had the discerning eyes of an eagle. He had eyebrows that needed some help, as they were rather unruly, but his beard was somehow well groomed and he rolled his large thumbs in a slow and confident manner. Like he was considering various options while listening to those who spoke and then he pulled out maps and pointed out the hills, the gulleys, the ravines where the Wehrmacht could be trapped. It would be difficult to explain to such a man what entanglement meant.

Once, at a meeting of teachers in Sabzic, where I went as a member of the local college students' association, he made a point that our country and our town was too vulnerable from the air and it was the mountains, valleys and forests that were our only defence. Only if Adolphus and his clowns retreated from the skies, could we think of defending Sabzic from the ground. This was not in the cards. In fact, he clarified that with the advent of the new German bombers like the dive-bombing Stukas and the Messerschmitt fighters, the Germans would be going for strategic bombing. Sabzic would become rubble. That was his analysis.

"No finely cut rocks, no well-hewn marble, no stained glass can be preserved—no Psalm, no Surah, no five books of Moses could save our country. Only the mountains, forests, valleys and our convictions, could."

With that assertion, he quashed any possibilities of debate. He was into clear-cut assertions when he did speak up.

Raid after raid of the Luftwaffe over London, Liverpool and other cities, however, had set England on fire. German intelligence about the location of industries pivotal to the war effort and war support did not seem to be very focused. Strategic warfare was probably not very important in their thinking, to win the War. The Luftwaffe was thrown into confusion as Himmler and Goering battled for Adolph's attention. I stood up and interjected that *Goering indeed was boring!* I did not actually mean that. In fact, Goering was quite crafty.

Everyone turned around to look at me. I thought I had broken the grimness, with what was a well-rhymed comment. Unfortunately, it was probably the first instance where the partisans considered my behaviour as irritating and bordering, once again, on insanity.

I was right, but on the contrary, despite the Blitz, Britain did not give in. Maybe because they did not have enough forests and mountains to hide away in! On the other hand, the carpet bombing of Dresden by the Allies, with no military assets or intelligence on the ground, broke the back of the Wehrmacht and destroyed the Fuehrer's morale. There was a certain random destructiveness, an overpowering desire for carnage that was seen as the necessary battle tactic for the Allies. (That was to be proven later in Japan on August 6, 1945.)

There you go! London, Dresden or Sabzic could not be compared. There is nuance in debating; the Doctor was firm about not trying to defend our town.

Having said that, Ben's Bo drew me aside and asked me very conspiratorially—

"How many tons of TNT would be required to keep the bridges and main entry points to Sabzic ready to be lit up, if required?" I did a quick calculation in my head, concentrating on the main bridges and gates to the town, approximating the weakest points of each structure and came up with an exact number, which once again had everyone turn their faces towards me, because of the enormity of the tonnage. I had simply included all the churches, mosques, synagogues—there were way too many of them along with the bridges—and roads leading in from the mountains to the island. When my total TNT count was further questioned, I explained. Several resistance fighters once again said straight to my face that I was a LUNATIC. Some others hissed under their breath, that I was a *ludak*. I then explained quite carefully, trying my best to not hurt anyone's sentiments, that I had included the religious monuments—as I was of the opinion that all destruction should be uniformly secular. Some of the churches being close to the bridge and in the main plazas near the bridge would come down unintentionally and therefore I felt that some mosques and synagogues needed to be brought down to enable a new dawn in our town and perhaps in our country, to avert the subtle hostility between the followers of different religions.

Everyone in the room registered significant disgust at my approach, even though they seemed to speak variants of each other's languages and were from different religions, were marrying each other, having babies with each other and were all opposed to fascism, nevertheless. Secular destruction, however, was an uncomfortable proposition. I thought I would give it a try. Raise the level of debate! So as to speak. The Doctor held back his smile, by pouting his lips.

"Godless bastard, that Shaf!"

I lost that discussion, but later on Ben's Bo came up to me and asked me quietly if I could give him the numbers, minus the requirement of destroying the religious institutions and places of worship. I gave it to him very quickly and he noted it down, as well.

★★★

An anthropologist professor in the college I went to, whose name escapes me, had suggested that in this region that we inhabited, the notion of neighbourliness was a tenuous concept. While there was a fair amount of inter-marriage and friendliness in schools and colleges and even in farmers' markets at the plaza, the chances of distinctly identifiable religious groups or nationalities living together in the same part of town was quite an uncommon possibility. After all the homilies had been exchanged, the gentle smiling citizens would cross the bridge and go to their part of the town to eat and sleep. There was never any seething anger, but there was some suspicion. It remained confined under the surface. Obviously, because the larger enemy was so repugnant, the hostilities were kept under wraps. There were no warring factions as such and those that wished to be collaborators did so quite overtly and lived in a different part of the country. Under the right circumstances, however, smiling together, holding hands and chatting was quite prevalent, and Muslim women having coffee together with Orthodox Christian men was still possible. Eating and drinking together and attending each other's weddings was quite prevalent.

The point that I had tried to make was that temporarily destroying towns, cities, buildings and bridges that were four or five hundred years old and handcrafted by extraordinary architects, artists, masons, visionaries (no doubt with a lot of fat in their egos) and specialized craftsmen was itself lunacy whether it was done from the air or from the ground. But no one seemed to understand and instead regarded me as the *crazy one*, when I provided the numbers for just doing that!

Chapter Nineteen

The scorn directed at my skills at calculating TNT requirements for various applications, although occasionally dis-
missed as being hilarious and at the same time useful
education, did not insult me. What the partisans needed
to understand was that resistance planning meant being
careful and cautious—to cover all bases and yet inject a dash
of art into the science of war.

In any case, amidst all the blood, bandages, stretchers
and burials, I had the opportunity to get closer to the fighters. And they were not all Christians for a start, as Ben's
grandfather would have deemed and nor were they all
conscripted Muslims, and for that matter some were pretty
daredevil Jewish fighters. They were furiously anti-fascist!
And amidst a smattering of all of the above, being able to
operate the radio allowed me special access to war news
from various fronts in Europe but as well as from Singapore
and China. This was quite exciting in terms of mapping out
my own thoughts and intellectual development in terms of
gaging all the possibilities of human-to-human relation-
ships—like for example conveying the ideas of the stalwarts
of Physics and Philosophy to the partisan fighters who were
having stale-bread sandwiches in trenches. I screamed out

postulations and proclamations about the progress of the War—along with Archimedes, Da Vinci, Galileo, Newton, Einstein and the more recent quantum physicists, while the rattle of Mauser machine guns came closer from time to time and then faded away. A symphony of entanglements that the narrow confines of trenches could not possibly accommodate. It is no wonder what they thought of me.

There was evidence of a steady decline of the forces of the Axis powers' military capabilities. I quietly conveyed this to our commander—the Doctor with various names. He understood. But my screams in the forests and trenches, which allowed me to ventilate, and which I rather enjoyed, made my fellow fighters begin to turn around in anticipation. It was like a stage. Was I doing it or was someone else doing it? They had smiles on their faces, as I explained in comical terms about Goebbels' latest lies, the London fires, Rommel beating a retreat or the reports of the breaking of the code in the Atlantic and then about our commander's meticulous planning as far as burying the Panzers by leading them on to ditches. He looked embarrassed and kept his head down, while all of us partisans leapt up and raised both hands in victory salutes. They were not the Sieg Heil type flat handed salutes that some in our country had taken up in support of the Axis powers. Ours were clenched fists.

Initially, after having overrun Western Europe and the entire Greek mainland, and then sweeping into our part of Europe, Adolphus realized he had to be quite disappointed with Benito's failures. On the other hand, Rommel and his desert warriors had swept through North Africa, belittled the British and were advancing on the Suez Canal. The Soviets were surrounded by the Finns and Germans, and Leningrad was under virtual siege. Millions of the Red Army had been wiped out or held as prisoners. They seemed to be unstoppable. Romania, Hungary and Vichy France and the benevolent neutrality of the Swiss and Swedish had made Adolphus quite cocky and his peacock strut had been greatly enhanced.

But! 1941 may very well have been the peak of German successes. Not only did they have to deal with Soviet and British arms production, the Americans had stepped in with their massive production capacity. As an example, when the Germans had produced 165,000 machine guns, the combined production of the Soviets, the Americans and the British and their dominions had produced over 1 million. Such details do not seem to register in the heads of war strategists. Effectively on, one thwack-thwack-thwack from a German Mauser nest would be followed by an endless thwack-thwack-thwack-thwack-thwack from the Brownings from our trenches. And the same followed from 1942 onwards, when it applied to aircraft and tanks. The sound of war was literally a victory roll of the success of the economic power of industrial production. But more importantly, the Germans had a problem with fuel. Romania and Hungary supplied a large proportion of their requirements and this was falling apart. Rommel, the legendary fox, was unable to lock down the British. A wily General named Montgomery held out against him in the Suez and Rommel went on sick leave. All this was coming through the radio. And I did not fail to write a few rhyming sentences to announce them. When I shouted them out in short bursts, the comrades promptly repeated them, one region to the next and it went through the forest like the howl of foxes and cheetahs.

Accuracy was not de rigueur. I would scream updates out when the sound of war would quieten a bit and my fellow fighters would applaud. There was a near rush of chemicals into my brains as I heard them repeated in the trenches and below the large trees in the snowbound mountains. From trench to trench the news would spread. That the Desert Fox had been beaten back. "The Fox is out of his hole." "He's been beaten back!" was the refrain. But what the rest of Europe did not always accept was that it was us partisans—nearly 800,000 strong—who had chewed up Adolphus' sagging posterior. No one was singing our praise in the rest of Europe.

While the Germans were getting devastated in the waters of the Atlantic—their code had been broken and U-boats were sinking everyday—and the Soviets had now totally surrounded the Germans and were picking them off one at a time, there was a huge battle where the partisans fought the Germans, trench by trench, in a little town a few hundred kilometres northwest of Sabzic. The German sense of superiority was something worth consideration.

I remembered an exchange with Nika.

I had written down some notes in my diary and as well in the margins of the book I had given to Nika to read about the Krupp dynasty. The Nazis like Ribbentrop, Rommel, Goebbels and Hitler himself were manipulators of the German self-esteem of a superior race. They used that, but as well played the hands of the big German industrial estates. Bo understood this very well.

"In the big War that lasted only four years, the German Empire was planning a major access to the Persian Gulf, because oil had been discovered on the Tigris Euphrates basin." My notes in my diary.

"Shares! Shares! It was all about shares!" Nika had again written in the margins.

The Krupp family and the Holzmann Construction company were big players, because there was steel, construction and infrastructure (buildings, bridges, tunnels) involved. The Ottomans were becoming weak by the end of the nineteenth century. They were in debt. The British of course would not allow such an advent of German incursion into the East. The British understood railways. They knew what railways were all about! Not as a people mover, but as a goods hauler. The Germans wanted to avoid the Suez and from the Bosporus, dip into Aleppo and then reach Basra. The Suez was controlled by the British. The Germans also wanted to avoid the big guns of the British around the Suez and so the railway line was designed to go through complex bypasses through mountains and long tunnels. And the money came by issuing shares. The shares were issued by the Deutsch Bank and the project was jockeyed through by a certain Georg von Siemens, who was on the Board of Deutsch Bank but also the nephew of the main von Siemens in the Siemens Industrial group. So, from Krupp and Holzmann to Siemens and the Deutsche Bank, the Germans had a plan.

Nika had marked it all up in the book I had given to her. She understood.

Chapter Twenty

I was nervous and suffering from a stiff back when I finally got into Zurich, by a combination of bus, train and finally a taxi organized by Ben's Bo. As per his request, I was to still change buses twice, even though I could have made it on the same bus, part of the way. He told me to travel light and so I only carried a rucksack. This was an important meeting.

This city was overwhelmingly complex, intellectual, ornately cultural and yet seething with counter-intelligence types. What I mean is that the Swiss have been quite shady in terms of their frequent assertions about their neutrality. Be it with the Germans, the Austrians, the French, the Belgians or the Italians, they have been quite suspect, as to neighbourliness. They managed to dodge bullets from all directions, despite some notable "accidents" but the peaceful neutrality of the Swiss was admirably militarized. With all that history of artists, poets, rebels and writers lounging around, and the money! An imposter would stand out.

Nika and I, we had planned a trip together to Zurich, but that never happened. She kicked off her shoes and lifted herself up onto the parapet alongside the canal. I held her waist and our tongues rolled inside our mouths. And she suddenly said *Zurich! Should we?* I agreed and that tongue roll and the teasing word Zurich shooting out of her mouth, left me with a sensation I could always bring up in my mind, whenever I wanted to and whenever I felt gloomy. We did not have the money to stay anywhere, though we could pay for the bus and train fare. So, stepping on to the streets of Zurich, I felt blessed and sad.

And yes, money! Now that MONEY had to be said with a hoarse but grim intonation, because that is the way the Swiss liked it. That is the way it was set up. But, besides the money and the private banks, there was the scent of Voltaire, Joyce and even Lenin who had passed by there, at some point. Either as drifters, political refugees or exiles. I would like to have counted myself in as one, except I was only a motherless physics teacher, on a secretive trip and a rendezvous with Ben's Bo, in a city I had no feel for. And he did. Because he was now considered a transnational resistance leader. A cosmopolitan man who had been around, since the end of The Great War. He understood history, the rules of social change and the topography of each nation. He called the shots, in a manner that was charismatic. Now in comparison to the village of Sabzic (and that is what I would define it now as—a village, after arriving in Zurich), I realized that things were done here quite differently. People spoke gently and smoked, with their eyes looking out pensively—kind of half open—and walked with no hurry, devoured chocolates with their mouths barely moving, rested on chairs on terraces with their hats on and sipped their coffee like royalty. And maybe they were. But what is royalty, anyway but inherited land ownership and intermarriage amongst incestuous landlord families, is it not?

And what a contrast the way elderly or middle-aged women walked about in this city! They wore short overcoats just above their knees, smart hats and high heels as they hopped over the tramlines, and in and out of large departmental stores. Some wore silk shawls, some wore sunglasses. Yes, there was war going on...but in my village, I would see women in dark overcoats and scarves around their necks, their heads covered, sheepishly looking at passersby as they foraged for edibles along the trails. They were bent over slightly as they trudged on alone.

I was intrigued, but unconsciously absorbing everything for personal use in the future. There was some merit to being standoffish and regal, even if you did not have a penny in your pocket. Never mind a pocket watch with a long chain hooked to your waist coat. If you had a beard, it had to be carefully coiffured till it was either like a never-used broom or a delicate paint brush that was continuously teased to a point of perfection. Yes, I felt a sense of inferiority as I watched, carefully, the walking style of the men. Slow and deliberate, but not casual. In Sabzic we rushed around like headless roosters and addressed each other like we were almost ready to chew or beat each other up, at any moment.

Zurich is a congenial city. Congenial to itself. It believes in a free, fair and democratic set up, as it smiles at all foreigners with money, because here you have the inherent creed of the Swiss to squeeze the dollars and pounds out of everyone and keep the franc strong. If the Swiss were eulogized as pacifist, it was probably because of their contrived neutrality as far as fucking everyone equally, that made them stay away from wars. It is a national ethos that is melted deliciously into the insides of each chocolate that I ingested while sitting across from Dr. Pyotr. They were bombed, by both sides, inadvertently or purposefully; but the Swiss made a demonstrative show of their air force skills by chasing German planes with German-made fighters. They did not do too well, but at least they were able to negotiate and maintain their neutrality. What a great city it could be after the War was over for a Physics teacher—to teach Art.

I found the house in an alley where he had arranged to meet. It was the second house up from the corner of the street, next to the big canal. Three storeys high with a polished red roof. The top floor exterior walls were painted dark, while the two floors below were predominantly white with some brick work showing up underneath the plaster. Around its sides along the alley there were some paintings of coil springs with the values of the spring force written up in carefully calligraphed formulae. Dada. I walked up the stairs and knocked on the brass latch and he stood there with his unruffled grace as he opened the door and smiled.

Our conversation was tepid, but at times he surprised me with some remarks that seemed a bit hostile. He first asked how I was and if I had met his wife recently. I said I had not, as I was moving from one unit to another, as commanded by my superiors. I had not really had a chance to go over to meet his wife or Ben.

"Very sorry about your Mum. She was a great mother."

"Oh! It's okay. Thank you," I said in my usual inept manner.

"Have you been curious about the way things were happening in our country and why I asked to see you?"

"*Bien sûr!*" I said. "I have been. But that hardly proves anything about my knowledge of the way the War was going on."

Obviously, he was opening up about his mysterious appearances and disappearances. But I had already satisfied myself that he was a clandestine hero of some sort. He turned his back to me and was facing a counter along the wall.

"What about skirmishes? Any actions?" He looked at me and the creases around his eyes were prominent.

"Yes, there were a couple. Ambushes. We don't know what happened. It was very fast. We blew up a culvert. And the fascists rolled into a ditch and we opened up on them. I had no problems with that. But we took a bunch of prisoners from one of their platoons. The rest fled across to Hungary. The prisoners, I don't know what happened to them. They were distraught and pathetic. Some we put in our trucks."

He stared at me for almost thirty seconds. He seemed a bit concerned.

"Was your training only in weaponry?"

"No, we do have planning sessions, which include familiarization with the topology, the forests and rivers, caves and various hilltops, peaks—how to find them."

For the first time I realized that as a teacher, I may have been better, even though I had been kicked out. He had no charm. He seemed to be taking out some aggression on me.

"Did you not receive any training in political theory? What is it that we are fighting for?" He sat down as he breathed heavily and seemed to be snorting a bit.

"Oh! I know what we are fighting against! Surely not just the Wehrmacht, and the Panzers as such."

"Right. So, what then is your opinion?"

He got up, turned around and grabbed his coffee and pushed a mug, which he had prepared, towards me. The plate had some chocolates on it. I took two or three. No point in losing this opportunity. But I did feel at that instant that perhaps I had been the cause of his daughter's death. Maybe that's what was going through his mind and he could not bring it up.

"We are fighting a political ideology, known as fascism. A culture of racial intolerance, but…"

I was beginning to get a bit irritated by his tutoring style. I did not respond. I did not know him this way.

"It upholds two things—extreme nationalism and extreme hate. It seizes the opportunity when there is an economic crisis and unemployment and grabs the attention of those who are ready with quick solutions."

"And then they say they are socialist!"

"But, of course!" He paused for a while and then went on. "Yes, of course! Like a wrench, they throw it in!"

He got up, taking a deep breath. He looked around and slowly turned around.

"You always seemed to fiddle around and walk in circles? What bothers you, most?"

Oh! He is going on the offence. Fiddle around. Now that is surely an insult of some sorts. He says this in a surprising change of manner. He was normally not very cold or pushy in the way he talked to me.

"I am not devious, if that is what you are suggesting when you say I *walk around in circles*."

"I did not say that. I do not play with the lives of people. Hope you understand that?"

He hesitated a bit. I was not saying anything.

"Do you? I had seen your interest in joining the partisans from the time you were teaching Ben."

"I am simply disturbed by the breakdown."

"Which breakdown?"

"Oh! In the piety of our beliefs."

"Piety?"

"That we are partisan fighters above all, and therefore the rest would follow. Kind of righteous. I do not think that way. Nothing is natural and automatic."

"So, you think fighting the Nazis should not be a priority now?"

"Of course, it should be. If we don't, the world will be changed. We'll be speaking German."

"So, what is the breakdown, my friend? Say it!"

"Because, as you said, the fascists rely on nationalism and even their own version of socialism and they cloak their hatred with that. It is obvious."

"So, what worries you?"

"I am not sure we have a basis for being united against them. On the surface, we have a big enemy on a blitzkrieg to rule the world."

"But?"

"I don't know. It seems we shame ourselves into fighting them. Not everyone is united in the same way. Some of us are seething underneath and would become fascists themselves."

"Yes, of course. We know that. Interesting! We have whole nations who have acted as collaborators, but think of it this way, despite all the wars, all the break ups and all the conflicts between religions, we have come together as a single nation, now. Have we not?"

"I do not think so. But I wish it was so. And you know what I am saying. We are not one!"

I looked him straight in the eye and he knew I was looking at his family at that moment.

He sat down for a while, took off his beret and ran his fingers through his hair. He must have been in his mid-forties at that point. I was still in my mid twenties. We both knew that there was confluence. The rivers had met. And that was good enough for the time being.

"Have you ever seen the gun?" he said, to break the silence. The gun? I did not reply. But I had an idea.

He went over and opened a closet and pulled out a double-barrel shot gun. The same one that Ben had talked about. The Remington double-barrel. He inhaled and then released his breath and Zurich heard that breath rushing through its alleys and street corners, like a wave that had a colour trace on it.

"This has traces of everything in it, the hand and foot-prints of several generations." He looked at it almost in a perverse manner.

He carried it towards me. I knew it was like a heavy piece of artillery. He lifted it to his nose. This was a different man I was seeing. He was not the quiet guy I knew in Sabzic. The inaudible father.

"It carries the smell of the fish from the river in Sabzic." Please do not go further!

"In which I swam and picked up, shocked and trauma-tized fish—blasted at, to make them rise to the surface. It is the gun that Nika got killed by. Do you know how it happened?"

"No," I say. "I don't have the details." My throat felt horrible.

"Well, he came over to our house and threatened Lana."

"Who did? The prosecutor?"

"True Blood!" he said, "True God! And that she was being a bitch, a whore. And he pronounced whore like she was an eel in a well, that sucked up the carcasses of prisoners who have disappeared. And he spat on the floor like he was a landlord. And Nika, heard it all and she rushed out with the Remington, fully loaded."

173

He sat down at this point and stared at the floor. The gun was still in his hand. Then he laid it down on the table and he picked up his mug. I now realized that I was going to find out more about Nika's death, which I had very few details about. In the trenches, he was called the Eagle. I thought he was like a Swallow.

"He came rushing over to Nika and she was about to shoot him. And Lana tried to stop her, and so did the demon!"

"So, was it an accident!"

"No, not really…yes, maybe…he tried to twist it out of her hand and that was when Nika must have pulled both triggers at the same time. The barrel end was facing the ceiling."

I did not care to listen to the rest of the details. And neither did he want to recount it. I stood up.

"Now this Remington must finish the job. Let me tell you one thing though. My family has had Christians and Jews marrying each other. When I met Lana in college, she was indifferent. That is why we got together. So, you would have been a welcome addition to our family. But, not so, as per my father. For him, it meant that 'true blood' would be adulterated."

"I understand." I looked at him with my head tilted but my eyes bore into his and I said that with some hesitation. But, for me it did not matter.

He then went back to the closet and pulled out the large zippered bag and put the gun in it and I saw it contained a box of shots. He sat down again and looked at me. I took a sip of the coffee and felt that I was on par with him somehow. He sipped his and looked me again in the eye.

"Take this back with you. When you arrive in Sabzic, you take it to this address." And he slipped me a piece of paper.

I felt I had arrived. The canal was blending into the river again. He understood me. He understood that the basis for fighting fascists was still fragile. He understood what I was saying. That mindsets had to change. The consciousness and the subconscious instincts had to escape the dominant instincts. And that would not be easy.

"Do we meet again soon?"

"Maybe, maybe not. But I will be around there. In the slopes and forests of our country. And we shall drive them out. You can be sure of that. We will never collaborate and besides, it is not just about fighting the fascists, it is about larger stuff, building a new nation, with different values. Now, you shall go to the meeting, which you are really here for."

With that, he locked the door to the apartment we were in and we walked down the creaky stairs together. It was past eleven in the night and the moon was sliding behind a house in the curving alley.

***

This battle to the north of Sabzic was a turning point. A large number of partisans fell into a trap and an entire hillside was surrounded. The Germans sent a barrage of mortar shells from moving trucks and all the escape routes were blocked off. A thousand partisans, at least, were taken prisoner. It was followed by the summary execution of a few hundred who had been taken prisoner. Ben's Bo was one of them. He was wounded in the stomach already and they did not waste too much time on him. That was the last I heard of him.

My insides were gutted when I heard the news. Another partisan, who had taken up my method of conveying battle-front news, shouted from a trench some distance away. *The*

Eagle has Fallen, he said. And, it was repeated from trench to trench in voices that were wrenched in anguish.

My heart, my muscles, my tendons became dry with the kind of remorse I could never describe. Striated? Like a rock face with no feelings. Stretched to the limit, till there was no more possibility of being stretched further. His leadership, his charismatic skills had surrounded our platoon with a warmth, a temperament that was both easy going and militant at the same time. We were fighting the Germans and as well their allies in our country and we dealt them blow after blow, in hit and run tactics, till the big push in which the mighty Wehrmacht finally turned tail. Ben's Bo was not there to see it. *The Eagle had fallen.*

June 9, 1943, it was. The big battle north of Sabzic, which was not recorded anywhere in the history books. I had it down in my diary, though. I carried the gun back to the address he had noted down on the piece of paper. It was a long trip, by trains, buses, walking through forests and eventually even a small boat. I delivered it as I had promised him. He had arranged for everything, thereafter.

I remember when he locked the door to the apartment in Zurich and I headed for the meeting. As soon as we had walked about one hundred feet, he dodged on to a side street, waved to me and disappeared. I did not see him again, after that.

Chapter Twenty-One

Well, the War was now over. Formally closed out. Handel's *Judas Maccabaeus* was now going to be performed without the revised versions that even Goebbels was uncomfortable with. Imagine the subtlety of excluding a people from mainstream society, by including them on a separated stage, so that they could be showcased and yet gassed with impunity, later.

I was back in Sabzic, looking for some means for survival. The idea of a multi-ethnic mosaic is a pious abstraction, but it was no longer captivating me, if it ever did. The scars ran deep. Thousands of mothers, grandchildren, nephews and fathers had been exterminated, their corpses left to rot in the gulleys along the edges of the roads of flight. Why should I feel like an exception? Millions had been experimented upon, reduced to bodies that gasped from every pore in them and then gassed to death—sometimes even in airtight transport trucks, shipped from Berlin. Smoke rose from chimneys and it rose from hastily constructed fireplaces in castles, where papers and correspondence were being incinerated. It was an asphyxiating odour of bones that smelt like glue on fire, or when hair gets lit up accidentally and blends with the smell of documents, which exude the smell of cellulose, cedar and propaganda.

"But, Ben," I said to his absent soul, "one brand of Christianity had resorted to absolutism and another brand was now going to exhibit its magnanimity."

"Well," he seemed to say, "the Ottoman Muslims, the Roma from the deserts of Rajasthan and the Communists from wherever, were not the offenders who butchered Jews. In fact, Jews and Muslims fought together, against Adolph."

And entire towns exuded the odours of Jews, Roma, Christians and partisans, as they burnt in solidarity. Entire cities and towns were flattened and destroyed, not only by the Axis powers but their collaborators and our own neighbours.

The actual details, by country, were not yet available. Of course, the Allies tastelessly emphasized their losses; the sacrifice of the eastern block nations and that of the partisans was ignored in the radio broadcasts out of London, Antwerp and Paris.

Sabzic, however, remained intact. The bridge, even though riddled with stray gunfire, remained like a symbolic record of a forgotten era of visions of a harmony that must have meant something to Diedar.

The three personal casualties of the War—my mum, Nika and Ben's Bo—gave me a unique chance to grieve in private. Now, I may be accused of being very clinical, but can you really paste your tears into a piece of paper, in a diary, for the sake of record? Can you really transcribe the pain you feel in your limbs and your head into the pages of an outdated diary, especially when you have lost everyone close to you?

Nika. She was not a direct participant in the War, but her head was quite clear about what she wanted out of life. She did not take her life. This I ought to make very clear. She was actually going to use the gun.

"Yes, Ben! She had loaded it fully and came storming out like a petrel. And she did end up pulling both triggers. She was sure she would not suffer the indignity that her dreadful grandfather had in mind for her."

The humiliation of being called a whore for planning a life with me, outside her creed, her religion (which I never figured out what it was, or if she had any allegiance to any, anyway). But in the end, things went wrong and my beloved was blown to bits. The blood was all over and Mrs. Ester had to wash it all out, her first born's plasma cells, from the walls, the bed sheets, the wooden almirahs, as she wept. Ben had just cycled back home. Mrs. Ester was in a frenzy. She chased him away. I understood.

When he came back, his life had changed.

And when he found out about his father's execution, Sabzic was no longer a comforting place. His nearness to his mother had been a blessing but had also become a sentence. He was not a child any longer. What would you do anyway in a place like that? It was so serene and modest that even the War could not destroy it. Some cities in our country and elsewhere in Europe were totally wiped out because their architecture was iconoclastic; they had institution-alized their history, their memories. There was nothing to wipe out here. Every building in Sabzic was modest, even the so-called palaces of culture, the museums, the courts, were all non-descript. Like any other building. Some of the synagogues, mosques and churches—Ah! yes, you could recognize the eras they were built in or modelled after—the architecture preserved some of the memories, but the city as a whole did not have the burden of remembering. Except!

179

The Bridge! It was a spectacle. The Bridge was not just a crossing point over a meandering river. It was a monument. So, why would anyone destroy the bridge in Sabzic? Ben's Bo had made that point. Why would anyone shell it from the hills, send bombers over to uproot its foundations, built by hand and glued together by molten lead? Why would anyone flatten this city? Was memory so offensive and inescapable, that even modest walls of stone and buildings of monumental innocuousness, should be demolished?

The War ended and the bridge and the mosques and the blue-domed cathedrals and churches remained. A mix of invasions and architectural memory, undefined, and a mix up of cultures that no one could put their finger on remained. That was enough for Ben to evict himself and go to a place where he could find uniformity of memory, architectural splendour and congruence and the potential that it could symbolize a departure from the hodgepodge that was Sabzic.

So, he went to college abroad and seemed to have settled down in the same city where I had rendezvoused with his Bo. Zurich—from where I had brought the gun back and delivered it to the address I had been asked to. It was a long trip over several days. But it did the job.

How the Bo was so shrewd! Despite his worldliness, his beliefs in the universality of the human spirit, his unbending beliefs in fighting fascists, he still found time to plan this personal odyssey to deliver justice, within his family, but not because of vengeance or anything like that—but to make the point, that what you do to others would come back to haunt you. I am intrigued by this saying, quite a bit. I suppose Ben would be too. Because it is there in all the philosophies, be it in various sayings of Jesus and his followers, the Hindu scriptures written some four hundred years before Jesus, in the Talmud, in Zoroastrian edicts, in all the Abrahamic religions and in Greek philosophy. What is the intent of it? Is it to discourage revenge? Is it to expect to be treated the way you treat others? Is it to expect being hurt if you hurt someone else? Is it to endorse the notion that fate always catches up with you?

Is it a good thing to not love someone back when the person carries out an act of murder out of extreme possessiveness and hatred? But retribution was on the Doctor's mind, for sure. He avenged my mother and his daughter, by disposing of his father.

About my mother. Without seeing much of my father in my life, I was close to my Mama—yes, I clung to her. And if she made fun of my teaching skills to Ben, it was only because she adored me as I reached the mid-twenties. I could not bury her. I cannot talk much more about that.

When I eventually met the elegant and extremely intelligent Mrs. Ester for the two-feet-high coffee and biscuits, she was quite on top of what was going on in the world. Although, she seemed a bit ragged around the edges, and her grand smile had somehow disappeared, her eyes were extraordinarily attractive in the way she introduced various topics for discussion. She would not bring up Nika, or the Doctor or even the fact that Ben had left town. She talked about something that I had not really kept up with, the emergence of the United States in the European theatre.

***

On July 12, 1947, the Secretary of State of the United States, named George Marshall, came up with a wonderful plan to rebuild Europe, she said. The continent lay devastated after the six-year war. Most cities were destroyed. Be it Warsaw, London, Berlin, Rotterdam, most of the large cities of Western and Eastern Europe lay in ruins. The Americans announced the grand plan, donating at least 13 billion dollars in funding for rebuilding infrastructure, railways, bridges, the production of food, starting up factories and providing support to education and the sciences. Of course, this was a grand plan. On the surface, she said. She had followed it closely. The Americans were clear that they would not allow a re-emergence of the same political atmosphere that followed the first War.

"But it means that American factories, that have grown exponentially as a result of the war effort, would also be in a position to supply goods to Europe. If trade barriers were lifted!"

She knew what she was talking about.

American management methods were also getting to be popular. And besides, the Cold War was rearing its ugly head. Churchill was soon to make his Iron Curtain speech. And the Soviet Union, although not at all pleased with our country, was considered a threat to the United States. All this to say, that it is never benevolence and altruism that makes the big powers spread their wealth abroad.

Mrs. Ester's eyes lit up when she told me that instead of waiting for the Marshall Plan to take effect here in Europe, I should, instead, head for the US and find out how that country was ahead of the rest of the world. She is the one who used the words that meant that one must *go against the tide.*

Seasons change and parched leaves drift away from forlorn trees. I thought it was a good time to stop staring at the leaves as they drifted further and further away from the tree. The gentle and fresh breeze enabled fresh green leaves on the highest branches. I looked around and realized that there was an absolute need to rebuild the towns and cities to their past heritage and glory. There was also a need for reconstruction of the minds of people. I did want to get back to teaching and into the future.

Unfortunately, grand ideas thought out by savants and well-meaning philosophers can sometimes be disrupted by the devil-dances of despots and their impish followers. Many other things happened as well, with several leaders in various countries declaring themselves as absolute rulers, immediately after the end of the War. But more importantly, many nations decided they must compete and win the battle of controlling economies and not necessarily embrace the lofty values that they had announced they would follow.

So, last week, I was waiting to meet an old professor at a coffee shop in Sabzic. When I went to meet him at the college, he said he was too busy. So, he asked me to meet him the next day. Was he afraid of meeting me? Could he have some reason not to?

In the last few months of the War, I was frankly transformed into a maniac. I went on a rampage. Something egged me on, deep inside. After the mass execution in the battle, north of Sabzic, I could not continue as a radio operator, or a TNT-requirements calculator. I climbed out of the trenches and planned ambush after ambush, following the lead of the Eagle. He had taught me how partisans should carry on the battle. It kind of came to me naturally. I had observed him carefully. He would lead small groups along the edges of the forests while the Panzers rolled along and then he would find a culvert and launch a diversion. Meaning, he would have gunfire from inside an old car (with no motor, nothing inside, salvaged from a farm) open up on them. Actually, there was no one behind the gun at all. It was a wire-controlled Browning and the Panzers would come rolling towards it and immediately fall into a hollow ditch, that was carefully dug up and covered with planks and hay. Then the Germans would get out and start helping that tank crew. That is when the women snipers took over.

There were many ambushes like this and once the Germans got wind of these repeat scenarios, they stopped falling for it. That is when I went into one of the cars and waited for them to walk by in a column. They were going to ignore the car. The hillside erupted and grenades fell on them from all sides and I opened up from inside the old farm cars. When I came back to our town, there were citizens who said I had fire in my eyes. That it is my upbringing that made me so mad. It is my religion that made me murderous. My religion? Really? Did I have one? I had a long beard, of course. In any case, it did not matter to me. The main thing was that the War had come to an end. But, did it? I mean the fact that we had all fought together was already becoming a fading memory. Is that why the professor was hesitant?

The professor did make the appointment. He bought me a coffee and asked how I was doing. I told him that I needed a job. He said there was none. He was matter of fact. He took a sip of our unique coffee, foaming over at the top, which he removed with a spoon, drank some cold water from a small glass, and then went back to the coffee. Then he cleared his throat, sat back and spoke.

"But if our leader was not hard-headed, we would get money from the Americans, to rebuild the colleges. And then there would be new teaching jobs."

The air was still. The confusion was paramount. What we had fought for was up in the air.

So, I kept coming to the coffee shop, looking for someone to buy me coffee. America was to rescue me. The message was clear. No money, no coffee. And the dry leaves roll away, without fail.

Chapter Twenty-Two

On January 1, 1946, Emperor Hirohito of Japan declared that he was not God.

It occurred to me that it was a good time for me to turn a new page in my life. The futility of World Wars was being felt in the sinews of most ordinary citizens. I was sitting under the sparse shade of a fig tree, by the canal, looking up at the stone bridge. It was pock marked with bullet holes and shell hits; its beige towers chipped away at the corners. Nevertheless, the bridge had managed to stay firm, despite the four-hundred-year onslaught on it during the rule of several empires. Dictators, sultans and zealots striding across its curved and arched soul, as they muttered religious praises and incantations of the superiority of their psalms and shuras. The fact is that even after millions had perished in gas chambers, in mass executions, in poppy fields and in snowbound battlefields, in dense forests and under the domes of mosques, churches and synagogues and in ghettos set on fire from the air, one would expect to question these hateful edicts that prompted such carnage and eventually some good sense would prevail. Those humans removed from the tension of battle and the excitement of killing each other and burying their own, would sit down for a long shot of coffee, or fresh Seville orange juice, face to face, and rethink a little bit about the hatred that fueled such wars. But wars are not fought for lofty values. Like sipping on a bitter blend of coffee, dipping toasted crumbs on extra virgin olive oil, the sunshine that makes you close your eyes and smile to yourself, love that makes you surrender so easily, the chirping sounds of a teal in a green field, and the spread of Algebra innocuously amongst young children as a way to resolve the most complex crises. So, despite the lime-beige colours of the bridge, brilliantly lit up by a setting sun that had temporarily enthused me, I looked away to the sides of the Strand and could not but look at the dour grey houses on the north side of the river where my mother had once lived. My head dipped and I realized that the question was not a matter of whether one felt godlike, or that one God had failed or another had succeeded. But that humans had failed themselves. How could one preserve one's sanity?

Two things happened in 1947. Or rather, three things.

One, I kept repeating to myself that I was not insane. Even though, I obsessed about being sane. As well, I was seeing Nika, now frequently. She appeared on the Strand, on the balcony of the apartment that I stayed in, across the street in Sabzic. Either she turned around and looked at me or she walked away gracefully. She wore a long dress, that was quite silky. The dress agreed with the wind as it flowed through her. There was an agreement there with the wind, her dress and the way she faded in and faded out. Sometimes I spoke to her very gently and she smiled. But she never spoke.

Second, President Truman declared the Truman doctrine of providing aid to countries whose governments were threatened by the possibilities of being overthrown.

And third, the Marshall Plan was declared.

You will notice that, so far, I have not commented on the latter two events.

Chapter Twenty-Three

It was June 17, 1950. Julius Rosenberg, a seedy-looking American scientist, was arrested on suspicion of espionage after having been named by David Greenglass, Ethel Rosenberg's younger brother, a former machinist at Los Alamos. On August 11, 1950, Ethel was arrested. Greenglass turned state witness and the prosecution's case was made solid. The execution was carried out for both of them on June 19, 1953, at a prison called Sing Sing. When executing Ethel, the first two electrical charges were inadequate. Her communist heart was still beating. Then they put through a heavier charge and smoke started coming out of her scalp. Now, these executions were not for murder. Just for being traitors, as the prosecution stated. From Picasso and Einstein to Sartre, Cocteau, Brecht, Frida Kahlo and Diego Rivera, all asked that they be pardoned. Their contention was that they had taken up a political cause and were not paid agents. At some point it was discovered that Julius had received $100 for expenses. A hefty sum indeed, for transporting atomic secrets and radar knowledge. This case ricocheted around the world because once the Truman doctrine and the Marshall Plan had been deployed, the tactics of pursuing the Cold War were formally accepted as fair.

Like a game of chess. The consensus in the United States was that if you were not with us, you were with them. In the rest of the world, it was somewhat different: while espionage was considered evil, it was widely practiced by all sides, but while one side felt virtuous until caught, the other side got caught and upheld it as patriotic.

When I arrived in New York City, a local daily reported that over 5,000 people reportedly of Russian origins, who had fled Tsarist Russia in the early 20th century, were rounded up and deported from New York alone, to the Soviet Union. Some of these folks did not speak a word of Russian and were immediately trundled-off to the Soviet Union. There were rumours that there would be similar deportations after the Rosenberg trials.

A letter from Mrs. Ester to me, after inquiring about my health, stated quite blandly that,

> When Wars end, prejudice surfaces and amnesia is invoked as state policy. Phobias towards other nationalities who did not exactly fall in line with the beliefs of the victorious nations become quite widespread. The back story is forgotten. This is what is happening here, so why not in the US?

***

I contemplated a life in the US nonetheless, and was determined to read about the scientists, the writers, the poets, the espionage trials and the slamming of protesters for being commies. There was political madness that could not be imagined anywhere else. How could I possibly miss out on this festival of craziness? The United States was also a grand celebration of creativity, science, innovation, entertainment, comedy and in general a proclivity towards massiveness in all things and gargantuan food consumption patterns that was intriguing to me. I went from city to city in the US. I was invited. Sometimes teaching, sometimes speaking as an invited speaker. My niche was to connect Physics with Philosophy and Art. Force and vectors with ideas and culture. I was also billed often as a "resistance fighter" in college posters and sometimes I started out well, but at some point, I had no clue how I would end. At times, I trailed off and there was no question-and-answer session. At one or two lectures, I got led away by the professors who had invited me to recuperate and be safe from my audience. Sometimes, they had to gently release me from my contracts, because I had embarrassed them.

All this resulted in a debacle for me and while I managed to stay on, thanks to colleagues in colleges, I had lost the ability to earn a living and gradually went incognito and became what is known as a *drifter*. Now this took a while. Almost three years. There were many Americans like me, hanging on to trains and trucks, going from city to city. They were out to discover their country. And at some point I stood outside museums where the elderly would offer me money and that is how I fed myself. Sleeping was not an issue. My rucksack had a sleeping bag and when it got dark, I rolled out my bed under a stoop or on a park bench and slept quite comfortably, except for the large rats in New York City who found the hole in my boots and nibbled at my big toe.

***

So, I am in a corner in Manhattan, I think. A swivel of my eyeballs to the northeast and an immediate roll back and I knew she was scanning me. People were watching her too, and coming to their own conclusions. But, minding their own business, I would say. From tall bank towers, security cameras on pivots with race bearings, turning like whispered secrets and through windows in cars, eyes were scoping me at a one-hundred-and-twenty-degree perspective. She caught my eyes and I looked away instantly. She pierced me through the cab's tempered glass windows. The cab had come to a halt, forty metres away. It was idling and dissenting; diesel engine rattling away, ready to discharge nuts, bolts, mufflers, crank shafts and the crabbiness only New Yorkers can understand.

Her eyes were fluid, on the verge of panic. The CO_2 was colourless in the air, emitting at the rate of nine times the gallons of gasoline that was being combusted.

I was just passed forty, I suppose.

Shadows stretched out on the broken side streets, where five roads almost met. New York is where the foreskin of the Flat Iron building protrudes out of the rooftop, and casts a shadow proboscis on 5th Avenue and you could tell the time on a bright sunny summer day on East 22nd, if you made the Flat Iron your gnomon. I know all this.

The day had gone by without incident. But now, her dark eyes had appeared and panicked and caused me some distraction. The traffic swept by, cars bouncing up and down on the uneven streets almost like in some rapids somewhere and I stood on the verge of control. She was looking at me. I knew that.

I had only so much time to look at her, in between yellow, black, purple, red cars and dark windows that rolled by like a movie in FF mode. But I am smart; I can make these connections between light, sound, moods and images while doing my job. And she was nervous, in between the cars, the blurs that went by, nearly hitting me with their rear-view mirrors. I smiled, lifted my arms, crossed them and moved my hips out of the way, in slender dance moves.

Albeit, I was a bit nervous, too. The hectic pace of maintaining the flow of traffic, a responsibility I had independently taken up, just in case someone accused me of dereliction of duty! But I could not risk dwelling on the same frame for too long. Several seconds later, two big tourist buses disgorged a full load of tourists and finally decided to move on and I had another chance to look. I noticed that the cab driver was totally unhappy that he had been asked to stop on a busy street corner, right near the end of the five-way crossing. Traffic was ripping down the road, a blur, like in a time lapse photo, as I swung my arms with significant craft, agility; hooting on my whistle with the authority that it deserved. There had never been an accident on my watch these past few weeks, on this corner. Never. Not even when I was not on top of the job, which did happen from time to time. The commuters, they all followed me and they respected my abilities. Thank you! America obeys, if there is someone to direct traffic.

She rolled down the window and got into an argument with the driver; then she opened the door and to my dismay she decided to cross the road. And car after car, raced by, clearly with no intention of halting for her. I stopped watching her. I can't take responsibility for the splatter that was about to happen. I must continue with my work. My task of directing this rather driven society, must go on.

She finally emerges from behind a car. I can hear a brake squeal. She is running to cross three lanes in leaping strides. Her hair flies in the air, spreading out evenly like a crown. A pharaoh or an Inca god or something like that is bounding towards the median. I watch her from the sides of my eyes.

Yes, she has crossed into the median, where there is a big yield sign. Now she will cross the small lane there for turning right. She is not looking. I am moving down the other median. I don't want to meet her. Because what is the point in saying hello to someone whose only trace left is a splatter on a wall behind a closet in a town called Sabzic? What will I say to her, in the middle of a median? I am scared. I start moving. She is not watching. So, I move faster. I am used to this. I know how to cross right through two-way traffic while the no-walking signs are on. I barely make it past when the red man is flashing and the green man is long gone.

She makes it across and finds I am not where she saw me, when she got out of the cab. I am in a parking lot, behind a bush. She looks shocked. She looks around in all directions. She waits for at least five minutes, sometimes walking a few feet and then coming back to the same spot. The cab driver, is looking at her. He has lit a cigarette and he is flicking the ash on the road. She has to cross back to the cab. She starts to cross and I leave. I am going to the back of the mall. I will cross the parking lot and then there is a loading station for the big eighteen-wheelers. There is a hatch door, just below the deck, which is locked with a padlock. Well, guess who has the keys! Now I start settling down in my living room and start writing in my black book, printed in Italy, which has on the cover a picture of a banana by someone called Andy. This guy is incredible. He leaves his sketches and paintings on park benches and with a soup can next to them. Folks pay five dollars or ten dollars and carry them away. Everyone pays. America is fantastic. Trust is fantastic. Watching from a distance is even better.

***

She and I played in a park somewhere in the old country. No, she had no grandfather, no serfs, watching us. No! It is not that girl. No! It is not Nika. I reprimand myself for bringing her name up, again and again, but less and less nowadays. When we turned twenty, we started touching each other. Before that we just played. I was sixteen, nearly ready for college, when one day we lay down in the grass, at the far end of the park, next to the canal and under the bridge. We knew it would happen. She put her head on my arms and my right hand slowly moved under her skirt. She did not mind at all. My hands travelled smoothly over her mounds. She was wearing a knicker that was not covering all of her. I left my hand on her and simply moved it around slowly. She kissed me on the cheek and then took my hand and brought it between her legs.

The fact that I don't remember her name does not bother me. Well, yes, it does a little bit. But I don't remember much else about her. I think her mother was widowed early. Her father was a racehorse owner. They had money. My mother had very little. My father had long disappeared in the US. He would send money. And that is how we were able to buy food, that we did not grow on the yard at the back of the house. We would wait for him to send for us. We had diminishing real wages and did not realize that. Which means our buying power, when adjusted against inflation, suggested that we should all be buying the cheaper carrots with rough skins and the soft, bloated tomatoes instead of the sculpted tasteless ones. But people nowadays do not follow their brains. Only our tactile instincts, which means we would buy the smooth carrots and tight tomatoes. All this to say that if the middle and working classes stopped catering to their image of themselves, they could put capitalism on crutches, because the margin of profitability is higher on the polished and shiny specials and so the diminishing returns part of the equation from high productivity is put in some jeopardy. But if we bought the soft tomatoes, the crisis could be accelerated because capitalism, as you know, digs its own grave by depriving its own workers of buying power and when the majority don't have savings, they don't spend and when they don't spend there is no cash flow and when there is no cash flow, everything starts to stagnate. And that is why on a daily basis, in the USA alone, eighty-one billion pounds of food is trashed, so that fresh produce can be decoratively placed to seduce the next day's consumer.

And then my dad got run over on the rail line over which the trains brought the tomatoes in cardboard boxes.

If she liked me, it was because I knew how to fly kites, make balsa wood gliders that flew steadily over our heads and dogs would chase after them and I would come barking at them and they would stop and scurry away. But the good thing was that this was a small town, with the mountains in the background, the bridge in the foreground and not much else. I don't know what agency sold Japanese Buddhists the idea of halting for a day at Sabzic! Sorry! New York. This is not a small town! And so, the Buddhists walked around looking bored; because after seeing Fujiyama, almost every morning, why would they get worked up seeing the discombobulated Adirondacks? They looked at each other and said stuff in Japanese slang, I deduced, but with polite disgust for the nation that had melted two of their cities, in an instant. Like, *"That's all? What the fuck is this? Did you get a rise? I sure did not. Did I miss something?"*

On a different note, in a small town like Sabzic the doctors are iconic. Like the school headmaster. Like the passage of an era, where a god with no wings, rests in town forever. So, I did go to see him about my problem.

My problem were these episodes I would have. They were pretty interesting, in the sense that I felt like I was high up somewhere, looking down and everyone had become ants and everyone moved slowly and smiled slowly and everything was dull and slow. When I told the Doctor, he said I need enrichment. This town was too small for me.

"What do you mean! I like our town."

"But, what can you do here? You need to wander. Visit museums, study art, talk to people for hours. Not walk in alleys, all by yourself. You will get into trouble."

"But what do I have?"

"Nothing. You are easily bored. Then you have delusions."

"But my head itches!"

"So, go clean it every day."

That's how I went to Faris, the pharmacist, and explained to him. He gave me stuff to fight scabies, even though I did not have any. I love to scratch my head. There are ridges in my skull, which I like to traverse with my long nails. Hard, so that I can cut a swathe through them and then it bleeds and I get scabs and then I have more to pick on.

That's disgusting. A friend of mine who studies History, said so, during one of our walks next to a swamp, where the moonlight shivers past the bullrushes and the water laps the sides of the embankment where we walk. I never come there with the girl. She would not know how to walk there. But with my history buddy, we can walk for hours, every summer, when we are back and it's hot and he wants to chat about the girls in his college. And I chat about the profs in Physics and we start another exchange on defining light, time and space.

"Go to a big college town. It will change everything. This town is too small for you."

The Doctor had said. The pharmacist had said so. My mother had said so. Lana Ester had emphasized. And now this historian with the eyes of an eagle, said the same.

Chapter Twenty-Four

On November 22, 1963, a man named Zapruder, fidgeting around with an 8mm Bell and Howell home movie camera, inadvertently shot a twenty-six second slice of the assassination of John Kennedy. He stood somewhere at the Dealey plaza in Dallas and recorded the possibilities of how coups d'état could be carried out without carrying one out, actually.

The film was analyzed to death subsequently and I happened to be in the United States. Nobody, including me, knew why I was there on that day. I just ended up there. There is a possibility that I may have been invited to make a presentation somewhere in Texas or New York, because of something I had written in an Italian Museum Journal about the cartilages running down David's left leg—the accuracy, the muscular tension and the swelling on his veins, resulting in a sculpted tension. That's it! *Sculpted Tension* was the topic of my presentation. All I can say is that, instead of talking about what I was invited to talk about, when I faced an absolute sea of young and eager students, I brought up the Zapruder film—my mother would, no doubt, have been embarrassed and would have had me thrown out for these acts of disdain—and I went on to speak about how the United States was such an omnipotent power already by then, that it could walk away from any incident without tarnishing its soul. It was entirely possible to enable the disappearance of several Prime Ministers or elected officials of several countries, and refer to it as a struggle for the restoration of democracy. No World War would result.

The two World Wars had also encouraged the leading powers of the world to imagine the possibilities of dropping TNT of far greater tonnage than that was done on Hiroshima or Nagasaki. Assassinations, overthrows, provoking domestic chaos through undercover operations made it much more feasible to orient the world to your bearings, rather than simply assassinate a Duke. No Benito, no Adolph, no Chamberlain was required. No goose stepping, no gas chambers, no hatred and even invasions of countries by the big powers was necessary. I think I finished the presentation at several universities and I did get some applause, but hardly any questions were asked. During one of the panel discussions, a nervous and agitated student asked if I knew that Goliath was a Palestinian. I said, he was not! He was a Philistine from up north. That was a strange question to ask me when I was simply trying to explain exceptionalism as a clever strategy. So, the craziness is not in me alone!

I think I blew it. It is Mrs. Ester who had egged me on to try out the United States. The skin on her face had lost all its tightness, but not the glow in her eyes. When I told her about my experiences after I went back, we had a quiet exchange. She poured me the two-feet-high coffee, while her hands shook a bit, in a glass, that had a chip on one side. The bone-china cups were missing from the cupboard in her kitchen. She did not serve any cakes or pastries. She had her head slightly tilted to one side, as she smiled and looked at me with a look like she was trying to remember the past. I had been seeing her from time to time to inquire about Ben before I left for the US. She squeezed her hands, as a way of controlling her emotions. I felt her embrace.

I asked her whether she thought that there would be another World War soon. Her words were crystalline. Drops. They fell and splattered on the palms of my hands and on to the earth below. Her anguish was mine.

"At some point, it will not be necessary to either attack or invade by the usual means to start a World War."

"Can you explain that, Mrs. Ester?"

"In fact, there will be no World Wars, but there will be worlds at war!"

"I think I know what you mean. Coups without coup d'état!"

"Yes, something like that. Well, we are going to be living in a world...soon...where the deepest secrets will be out in the open in no time. And ordinary people will have more access to news than listening to shortwave radio as you and the Doctor depended upon. Starting a World War will not be that easy."

"But it takes just an incident to start a war."

"Yes, but not for long. Wars will not be declared. The old style of conquering by physically invading, may not be necessary. Small skirmishes will happen. Incidents will be preceded by months of careful planning and subterfuge. Rumours, false news and sometimes staged incidents would be good enough to groom the mindset of an entire nation."

"And we will become so primed, that hatefulness towards others will come naturally."

"Yes, and it would be easy to forget and impossible to remember the past and live together as before. Have your coffee. Do you want some sugar?"

"Ah! No! Thank you."

"And I can see that already. The same words and same expressions are repeated by the news agencies. As if they share a common news source and they repeat the same words, non-stop."

"Goebbels had it right, that if the media repeated the same slant and the same words over and over, a desert could be transformed into a tropical paradise and vice versa."

"Have you heard from Ben?"

At this point, she left the room and came back with a picture. It was Ben, holding a baby in his arms.

***

After two years or so, teaching, drifting and restlessly wandering in the United States, I came back to Sabzic, or thereabouts, and realized that I had lost the apartment I had. So I went back to Zurich, where I had once been given a course to teach in an institute where Art and Science were taught with equal verisimilitude. They had no use for me. I understood that perfectly. The result of being displaced from my country and being unable to find employment, I roamed around, living like a monk—either asking passersby for help, or finding refuge under bridges and culverts. This was a dark period that ensued. I never stopped putting chapters down in my diary, though. I had heard that Ben, who was by now a practicing corporate lawyer, was looking for me. So, I stayed around in Zurich for a while. But my vocabulary had changed. In the few years that I spent in the United States, I had picked up new words, new slang expressions that definitely confounded fellow citizens under the bridge. And then she would appear everywhere. I had seen her in the United States. Now I would see her in Switzerland.

I was going to carry on doing my thing. Let things go, you know. I will not look at her. I will continue to do my work. I will lick my finger, stretch out my arms, watch the end of my fingers, beyond which lies the horizon and I will look at what is at the end of that horizon—and what will I see? In this case a curved road leading up to a lake and a lineup of stores along the side and I will point my finger at each store—like they are on my gun sight. Then I will go back and forth just like you would on a view finder from a distance while sitting on the rooftop of a big brown building that sits squat like in the Zapruder 26-second film on Jackie grabbing a piece of the President's skull from the back of the Lincoln. I would pick them off one at a time on my crosshairs, like the ricocheting zing and the dull thwack that registered the assassination that was never solved and the whole world knew it happened and there were no answers, still. It was the mother lode of all unsolved conspiracies, the very first psalm to be set to prayer. You don't even try to understand what certain nations have decided, by themselves, as to their role in the world. And I see at the end of my fingertips— nails, dirty and crusted with blue green material—that there is a sushi shop and I will certainly discuss the Japanese economy as well, if you wish, as the fantastic capability of Japanese management styles to mix teamwork and applaud worker heroes while stressing them out totally. I will not look at her.

Oh! But she has opened the door of the car and her legs are out! She keeps popping up, like in a film by Visconti.

Sushi and Kennedy never met really, although sushi was already big in the United States. Because he was too busy sniffing up the muffs of every Hollywood lass that came by his viewfinder and that is why he had Bobby, as Attorney General, clearly sanitizing around his mess and behind him, or calling up police chiefs to drop investigations which is what I would do, frankly, if my brother was randomly sleeping with a speckled horny blonde every other day, with mistaken notions about how far she can go, skirt billowing, with all the beauty spots in her body. And my nails point to a bike store in the same strip mall and next to it, as I squint my eyes just a wee bit, I see an alley there. And beyond the alley I can see in the distance a mountain rising; and when I squeeze my eyes, I can see that there were partisans walking down those trails, some twenty years ago, not here, but in an adjoining valley in a nearby country, lurking around amongst the pine trees and of course I won't get into a discussion about their notions of building a new country. And have a coffee together. But that part is over.

She has now closed the door and is out of the car.

But out there is where I should be. Not for sushi or the bike shop or the accountants' temporary office next door, because out there at the foothills of the mountain is a jungle where berries once grew, where red ants roamed, climbing impolitely over each other, where partisans crouched and I walked with them till they gave me a grey tarpaulin to sleep on, in a beetle-fly infested jungle where the best medics are the partisans themselves and when I got to talk to their leader, who is a doctor, I will tell him that the Kennedy assassination should have been solved—then his work would be done and he would ask me why I was making such a stupid statement and who the hell is Kennedy?—and how would that affect his campaign to get rid of the Nazis and I would patiently explain to him ("been there, done it all" was a favourite expression I had learned) because by then we would sit down on a moss-laden rock—my khakis would get soiled more—and then far away from that strip mall, we would start the discussion on how a certain concept of market economics had morphed into a political philosophy that espoused that the survival of the fittest, is the best domestic, and as well, foreign policy. So that when you dangle carrots in front of the people, and emphasize that only the fittest will survive, well everything else would follow. A coup d'état does not have to be a real coup d'état.

But! There has to be a plan. For example, if you do not have control of Iron ore, Copper, Nickel and Rare Earths, automobiles won't ply the highways you have built, and electricity would not be transmittable. And once you have automobiles, you need fuel!

If you don't have a plan to control the world, like a document, like a manifesto, or a dream of a new empire, a world order, if you did not have an economic strategy and a conspiracy in the works, you could not make your case for exceptionalism. Exceptionalism is simply sexual, like swagger, which also has to do with domination. But that is normally between two people in the moldy confines of a cardboard box inside a storm sewer in the city where night descends and a falcon with yellow eyes, that gently settles down for the rats and mice below, to panic or go into a freeze, as the falcon studies everything with a cold stare. There can be sex between nations, but there still has to be a conspiracy, a document and a plan, a falcon watching over you. I write, as the candle flickers in the sewer. I write, as she appears and disappears. The falcon watches.

***

I will not look at her. I don't want to look at her. I don't. I don't want her to cross the street. Someone please tell her not to cross the street! I am totally immersed in the traffic, but I am not and so I will talk some more, while the silly girl continues to cross the street towards me and the cab driver is pissed off and spitting on the street. What city is this? Why is she still headed towards me?

On June 5, 1968, Bobby Kennedy was killed. But I was already safely back in Sabzic.

Section Three

From Dusk to Dawn

Chapter Twenty-Five

"I shall see you," he had said.

"When?" I had almost snapped at him. He was surprised, but smiled at my impatient response. He knew I was expressing a fairly high level of resentment.

"Soon. Don't worry!" I forced a smile and looked at him. He winked and dipped his head, as he went through the door.

I never saw Bo again. His body was never found. It was thrown into a trench by the Germans along with hundreds of other corpses. They prepared a mass burial, after the big battle that took place a few hundred kilometres north of Sabzic. A young partisan had done the usual thing of playing dead, till night fell, and then he had jumped out and slipped away, bleeding, to recount the battle.

He was able to reach a village on the outskirts of our town and had sent word to my cousin who lived in the house where I had been sent to when Nika died. My cousin and her partner brought him to her house and treated his wounds. They were not serious. That is how we found out about Bo. The boy had seen him get wounded.

But, Shaf knew as well. He had managed to escape that battle and went on to carry out several ambushes, leading units himself. And then he was exhausted and the War was soon over. Shaf's tenacity, according to the young soldier, was out of this world. He was like a driven man. He would never stop organizing small guerrilla units and was setting off land mines that left an entire Panzer division in disarray. According to the partisan, Shaf had become a guerrilla hero. He maintained that one must never fight them in the open. Quick and decisive attacks and then just disappear, as soon as you can. If you had to stay, then lead them closer to the ravines and the ditches. He had learnt it from my Bo. Women partisans would snipe at them to attract them in, and the Panzers came rolling in and started to roll into the ditches. When you ambush the Panzers, from the sides, it is suicide. They would turn their turrets around and blow you away. He would not have that. He asked the snipers to ping them from the ditches and disappear. Then the Panzers would come rushing in and in no time got demobilized in the ditches, or blown up. According to the young partisan, Shaf was a man on a mission, fighting the Nazis. He led one combat mission after the other, but he always planned them down to every detail. Very few knew his name. Only my Bo knew he was called Shaf by his mother, and our family. According to the partisans, they called him David. Or, maybe Daoud.

My Mama did not sleep for two weeks. The bulges under her eyes were swollen and dark. I did not sleep for a few days. Then I realized that it was time for me to look after my Mama. She had not eaten for almost a week. I started cooking eggs and boiling potatoes. I also made stews with beets from our backyard. There was no bread, until my Mama made them again. So, I went to the house of a neighbour and she had made flat bread. I was asking her if she could make some for Mama. She just gave me a basket of her own.

I came home with the bread, tossed the basket to the side and started howling, finally. It was an explosion that I had not anticipated. My Mama came rushing out and held me.

We stayed like that, holding each other. When I had stopped sobbing like a child, she said, "It is time for you to head out. The War is nearly over."

And so, I thought of going to Switzerland. I had heard about Zurich so much.

Like my mother, I went to a Polytechnic first and started working on a career in the trades. But that did not suit me at all. In the back of my mind was the need to meet Shaf, and unlike him, I did believe that there was a purpose in life and there was merit to believing in the rule of law. So, I went and collected several degrees and got swept in to law practice. The walls of the College, the walls of Zurich, the alleys, the apartments where my Bo had roamed and lived and where Shaf had also hung around, lured me away from Sabzic and my mother.

Chapter Twenty-Six

In our part of the world we had a thing about stone bridges, often built with an iconic intent. Like bridging two religions, two peoples and two aspirations. The Swiss had a different notion of bridges. Our bridges reflected the centuries of visits by Vazirs and Dukes who brought their music, their marching soldiers, their religions, their eating habits, and their plans to live together. But they also brought along their not-so-well-concealed apprehensions about living with each other. So bridges had to be permanent or be maquettes of the real thing!

The Swiss built wooden bridges that often caught fire. Shaf would have been delighted not only to study these bridges but by their vulnerability. If I knew where he was, I would ask him to spend time with me and he would endlessly lecture me on the futility of wooden bridges. He would probably say that they are purely ornamental. For solo evening walkers to cross over to an island on a wooden bridge. Perhaps, there would be a little museum in the middle and then you could come back and have a coffee. There were some other Swiss towns and cities which had chapels in the middle of the waterway. At least that served some purpose.

I was crossing the wooden bridge and the idea about *common space*, swept through me.

I kept questioning myself as to what lay at the root of nationalism and I answered it myself by using the word RACE. This word had now become a near plague. An infectious construct that everyone around me wanted to emphasize as a part of natural self-image. And when it came to publicly stating your identity, no one bothered to say that they were teachers, scientists, lawyers, stevedores, workers or refugees. They would say they were Ethiopian Jews, Latvian Catholics or Druze Muslims. In some cases, they would say they were Levantine Syrian, or from al Mashriq, where the sun rose in the East! What mystification! What was missing in all this was even the slightest enthusiasm for variety. Like eating together, in spite of!

Whatever be the case, the elderly, in their eighties still hung out together, smiled and talked about making weld repairs in shipyards, playing football together, repairing plaster on church walls and eating together! And attending each other's weddings! Bridges were built in Europe, mostly for people to cross over or just plan a meet on the bridge itself.

And when I heard about where our country was headed, I realized that my grandfather Marcus had actually prevailed. While the rogue had not planned to demolish the bridge and forever segregate one community from another, there were constant discussions that the famous stone bridge at Sabzic had to come down. It was old, cars could not pass, it was an eyesore and it had lost its meaning.

Chapter Twenty-Seven

Everyone in our family was naturally prone towards being matter of fact about every serious turn of events and for a long time I was caught in that temperament, as well. Things just happen and the faster you recover from them and manage to get up on your feet, the better it is for your health. This was a pattern of behaviour that both my parents inculcated in us. Being reserved about tenuous situations and not reacting in an obvious manner was considered a character trait. When bombs fell and mortars shook our windows, we were taught to be calm.

However, there was that one occasion when my mother went berserk and chased me out of the house. Her eyes went from demure and pleasant to being terror struck and help-less, with the whites bulging out, larger than I had ever seen and the red capillaries, ready to explode. I can describe this with aloofness now, but I could not imagine losing a twenty-some-year-old daughter in that manner! I did not realize the violence and intensity of that moment, when Nika pulled the triggers on the Remington. It was something for which there was no record. No photograph, no report. No evidence was left. Only my Mama and the monstrous Marcus had the images in their mind. All I remembered was the evidence left behind by the missed stains on the stucco wall at the top of the wardrobe and the strange washed smell in the room.

In all other situations, a tranquil, serene atmosphere prevailed soon after an event. And that included the frequent departures of my father. My mother stuck her face out from behind a curtain, like a despairing marble statue, as my father casually packed his rucksack and departed, every time. He dipped his head, winked and the sound of a casual click of the tongue, and a partially twisted lip, ended these short encounters. Then the curtains behind the door, called closure by gently folding back on their own. The curtains had a complimentary intelligence, as opposed to our family's subdued and suspended tenor. And calm prevailed.

My sister Nika, however, did not display such impassiveness, though. She often flew into a rage or danced through the air and landed on my father's lap, whenever she wanted. On some rare occasions my father gave me a hug, when I was desperate for answers. So, when I decided to leave Sabzic, my mother serenely said that it was a good decision. That was about it. In a strange sort of way, it made me escape this grippingly exciting family setting, where walking away mattered so much and the alternative need to be occasionally exuberant, was totally forgotten. The exception perhaps was when Shaf arrived twice a week and provided unintended entertainment for all of us.

My cycling expeditions were exhilarating of course, and I smiled to myself as I went through my exchanges with Shaf in my head, as I biked back over the bridge. The more I thought about our conversations and understood what he was saying, the more I was relieved. Nothing mattered more than finding him again and just holding his hand. After all, by now it would no longer be a teacher-student relationship. We would have become friends. And when I heard that he had become a planner for ingenious guerrilla actions, I wanted to have greater exchanges with him.

More than thirty years had passed. Perhaps, I would write a book about him. The insane guerrilla partisan from a land of many mountains and bridges. But he had quietly moved into a thin dimensionless air. He had gone to America. That is what my Mama had said. Then she said he had come back.

During my visits to various cities in Europe as a part of my work as a lawyer or sometimes to see my mother, I would plan and allocate some time to meet with lawyers, officials, academics and artists who had known of him. It was a very wide net I had cast into an open sea, hoping that I would find some traces somewhere. Sometimes I went to Germany, sometimes to Brussels, Munich and Paris. Wherever my job took me, I took a weekend off to meet exiles from Sabzic. My pretense was that I was writing a history of Sabzic. It was not just Shaf that I was looking for, but also my Bo. Some trace, some story that I could pick up. While I was more or less convinced that my Bo would never reappear again, I felt that Shaf still lurked around behind trees, sleeping under a bridge in a small town or teaching in an obscure college somewhere. I despised those who were possibly sitting in on his courses, for they understood very little of how his mind worked.

I did not know his family name. My mother did not either. In fact, I did not know his full first name. Nobody knew much about him. Shaf was like a dismembered shadow. Like a cartoon character in a family album.

Did he use a nom de guerre? My wife, Hita, understood my desperation to find him. She had listened to my encounters with him. My long exchanges on vectors, gravity, observations of moving entities, the physics of stress and tension, the impact on the physiology of the body and thereby its reflection in art and culture, all this made her intensely interested in this Shaf character, who remained radiant inside my head.

Hita decided to research all faculties in all of the countries adjoining the Balkans.

"I know you have to find out whether he is dead or alive. I am fully aware of that. He is one person in your family, whose departure is not very clear."

And it was she who had tracked down a professor, who had been teaching a course in Florence solely on David's missing muscle, on his back. Which was incidentally an irrelevant issue, because Michelangelo had clearly stated that it was true, as he had run out of a single block of marble from which he could cover the entire work. Hita had found the writings of the professor, who had taught for several years on this single subject. Michelangelo's David. Shaf had repeatedly asserted to both me and my family that David was not only a work of art and an astounding replication of the male physical form, but also a boundless creation of a rebel, gripped with terror and tension, as he steadied himself for a duel to death with Goliath. The tension in his mind was transported into his every muscle, cartilage, vein as he calculated the single blow that would knock Goliath down.

The professor in Florence was known to be a recluse. He was not seen after classes and when he appeared, a certain silence prevailed and carried on as he delivered a

217

monotonous three-hour lecture with a plaster model and projected slides.

It also turned out, as per his course material, that he propounded the theory that the killing of a Goliath by a David was actually a careful rewriting of a real incident into a fictional masterpiece from a chapter in the Hebrew Bible, Samuel 21. This made him quite controversial. In several accounts from this Bible it was apparently stated that the real slayer was a lad named Elhanan, son of Jair. But, as history is often a reconstruction from orally whispered stories (without exception in every religion), which are then transferred from lips to lips till they reach a scribe's ears, it was evident to this professor that Elhanan's name was slowly erased or relegated to a secondary role and was assigned to the killing of Goliath's brother, Lahmi. And David, considering his later role as a King, required that this heroic act be on his curriculum vitae. This part of his course material pointed to historical inaccuracies in Samuel 21, because in earlier chapters it was Elhanan who had done the job. But the well-intentioned scribes gradually shifted the credit to David, leaving the earlier chapters intact. That anomaly was never questioned, but this professor in Florence harped on it with significant emphasis along with his extraordinary lectures on the cartilages in David's thighs. He had one whole lecture dedicated to the minuscular size of David's genitals, which he explained was a typical result of extreme stress, tension and thanatophobia. Of course, academic jurisprudence did not immediately require that the inaccurate and possible manipulation of evidence be questioned and the embarrassing inconsistency be brought out into the open. Thus, the scribes deftly suggested that Elhanan killed Goliath's brother, Lahmi, and David's extraordinary heroism was added on to his other attributes as King.

The professor's contract was however not renewed and he was effectively terminated. And he retired to a small hilltop residence near Florence and was never heard of again. His name at the University did appear as a Professor S. David. It was of considerable interest for me to meet him.

***

The driveway was made of gravel and it took you straight to a carport. There were no other cars there. The reception was well prepared. Only one person at the front desk and he did not look you in the eye. They had everything ready and they knew that this flight brought in a lot of weary travelers late in the evening. But tonight, I was the only one coming to this hotel in this little town, ninety-five kilometres from Florence. He handed me the magnetic key, again without looking me in the eye. I took the elevator at the end of the hallway, as directed, and walked the long corridor to my room, dragging my carry-on over the narrow carpet. I took off my shoes and collapsed on the bed after the short flight from Zurich. I must have dozed off and when I woke up, I looked around the room.

The wallpaper in this second-floor room was a dark ochre. Tiny white flowers with silver tips dispersed evenly. An oil painting of a child, in a dark jacket leaning on one knee and staring at a reclining woman on a chaise lounge, hung low over the head-board. The wood in every part of the room was dark, but polished. And on top of each piece of furniture, table and sideboard, cold grey marble with dark grey veins running sinuously and the contours handsomely formed and fitted on the wood. A shimmery lace curtain hung sadly from the ceiling to the floor, on the window that faced the front street. The light coming through was easily swept away by a tug on a gold braided rope, attached to the wall and a red velour curtain would come down and assure absolute darkness.

The floorsboards were quite uneven, covered with a burgundy carpet that did little to suppress the irregularities in the floorboards. I lay down on the bed and threw the garishly golden bed cover over me. I left the door to the little anteroom open. The room had a sink in the corner and a little fridge poised on the marble table, asking to be invaded. I was not interested in its contents and it seemed like an obtrusive token of modernity in the morose and ornate style of the rest of the suite.

In my tired state of mind, I figured that the antiquated table lamp must have been conjured up by either a gothic-inclined Orthodox priest or by a Napoleonic order.

At about 2:37 a.m., I must have been quite awake when a soundless presence registered itself. My eyes opened and closed immediately. The Prince had appeared at the door. I did not move and while my eyes seemed shut, I could see him through my thick eyelashes, as he stood at the doorway. Ashen, with a reddish glare coming from his vinegary eyes, he kept looking towards the bed. I knew it was him. He stood there for a while, without a movement. He did look despairingly thirsty and then without hesitating, he pivoted around, his long coat flaring. Then he opened the fridge and popped open a bottle of San Pellegrino and poured it slowly into a glass while he glanced back at the bed. The fizz echoed through the room and I remained motionless. He then stepped back, settled down at the desk with his back to me and started writing. At this point, I opened my eyes and noticed he wore no socks, but had wrapped a long piece of red cloth around both legs till they reached his bloodless ankles. He had not taken off his jacket, and so the glow around him was fearsome. Nothing diabolic, though. I could hear the scratching of the nib of the pen on the paper, as he wrote with resolve.

I came to know that he would do this every day, every night and with every chapter he unveiled the basis of immorality as a force for good. His general philosophy was that for glory and survival, Princes, Dukes, Barons and writers of court history could deploy means that were far from moral. Morality was relative, just like observation was a temporary record. I broke out of that sweat storm that swept through me and I rolled over. And then he was not there, anymore.

But it was here in that room, he had slept, when he could, under the watchful eyes of a government he advised. And it was here that he devised the notion that everyone gets what they want by necessary acts of immorality, betrayal, fakery, espionage, subterfuge and debauchery. Comprehensive accomplishments and happiness can be brought about by acts of minor evil. The end could justify the means.

The hotel brochure stated that Niccolo Machiavelli had lived here in this building, 400 years ago. He prowled the long corridors outside, around the marble pots and the tiled walkways that led to a fountain. He came back at night to record his thoughts. He had a mandate from the chancery of Firenze and when he could get down to his acute cynical gifts, he would needle, prod and ridicule the positive in polemical debates, and went on to conceive the concept of a state that thrived on killing bright ideas with sharp slices of cynicism and offered instead malevolent twists to turn the tide away from the obvious. Or, could it simply be that he had a fascination for coups d'état when the calm got too oppressive?

The Prince was in the works and so was the play, *The Mandrake*. But, somewhere in there I was convinced that the world had come to be what Machiavelli had conceived. A diabolical state of trade-offs. Shaf walked in and out of every chapter. The obvious was an illusion and manipulation was standard. The clerk at the front desk, without looking at me, had given me some directions on a map.

***

In the morning, I felt a nip in the air and put on a leather jacket that Hita had presented to me last winter. It had fairly heavy padding all around and proved to be quite beneficial, in an unexpected way. I fetched breakfast from a sunny room downstairs, including a small flask of coffee and headed out to the point of rendezvous. An assistant in my law firm had tracked down the retired art history teacher, as per the leads provided by Hita. He had some similar behaviour patterns as the man I was searching for, for over three decades.

When I knocked on his door, in the small house on a hilltop that he had retired to, I was embarrassed to find out that only the letter for his first name was a match. It was Sergio. An elderly lady who was wearing an apron, opened the door, very slightly. In my broken Italian, I asked if there was someone named Professor Shaf living there. She looked behind her and seemed to suggest to me with her eyes, to get away as soon as I could. I did not have the instinct to run away immediately and so I backed off slightly from the door. A dwarfish looking, pudgy-faced man, asymmetrical and listless, with a mole on his forehead, emerged from behind her. He wheeled himself in front of the lady, shoving her aside. The man had no time for me and he did not even let me start my well-prepared introduction. He had an air gun on his lap and he was readying himself to point the gun, while maneuvering his rickety wheelchair. I spontaneously decided to decamp with all the energy I had. I ran backwards several feet and then turned around to run towards my car. That is when I felt some pellet-like impacts on the back of my leather jacket. I reached my car and raced away. In the distance I could hear *Tua madre è una puttana …a calci in culo!* repeatedly, as I drove down from the hilltop. Instinctively I felt a deep injury to my mother. When I reached the hotel, I felt an irritation on the back of my thighs. My jeans had somehow been unable to withstand the pellets and while the bruises would disappear, the wounds would not. Hita's heavy leather jacket had done a great job protecting my back.

Chapter Twenty-Eight

Two men with wrinkled faces, bemused looks, sat across from each other and slowly lifted their short glasses of black coffee. Both then popped a cube of brown sugar under their tongues and then the simmering coffee gently flowed past their lips into the dark interiors of their mouth. They smiled. The sun smiled down at them.

"That was good," said Mr. Partisan A.

"Ah! Yes," said Mr. Partisan B.

A flight of pigeons settled down on the pavement.

In front of the two wrinkled men on their plates were two ribs each, which they had chewed down to the bone. One had left half a potato on his plate. They both smiled and said cheers. A had no front teeth. His eyes bounced light in a magnificent manner. He had a dusty kippah, which barely clung to his nearly bald head. B had nothing on his head. When they finished their coffee, they laughed in the most infectious manner and finally stood up to leave. The one who had nothing on his head pulled out a small white skull cap from his pocket with embroidery on its side and fitted it on his head. A and B crossed their right hands over their chests, bowed to each other, hugged, smiled again and walked away into two different sections of the town.

I was sitting by the fountain, looking at them. Eight hundred thousand partisans had come home to build a new nation. Surely, they should succeed.

***

In Sabzic, before the War, I was told that weddings were for sharing meals. There were no restrictions when eating together. My parents cooked at home and we got used to desecrating many religious edicts by secularizing all meats. Irrespective of the religions that were followed by each sector in our town, when it came to eating together, not too many rules were followed. It was the exchange of the rabble. Incoherent to outsiders but intrinsic to the mood. Eating each other's meats and the rules of what followed the other, dairy before meat or vice versa, and using washed utensils etc. was tossed out and drowned out by the slapping sounds of lips smacking against each other. No one bothered to listen to each other's personal commitments about the sacredness of the food protocol. Weddings were a perfect venue to flout and forget all restrictions. In fact, in some neighbourhoods, people even ate from the same large plate. I had clearly remembered what my Mama had said. The act of sharing food together, and not eating alone in the confines of one's own home as per one's religion, was considered quite natural.

Before the War ended, when I biked around the plaza and the fountain and around the bridge, elderly people were not seen sitting together and if they did, it was their wrinkled faces and distraught foreheads that was obvious, and there were no legs of mutton visible on the table in front of them. After the War, even women joined together on the same table. Not everywhere, but often enough that it was noticeable. Outside in the cafés, occasionally Muslim and

Catholic women sat around and had coffee together. This was noticeable. As a teenager, it did register.

I pondered over these issues, and years later after graduating from college, I read through nearly five hundred years of history, of empires battling against other empires and the resulting impact on law, bureaucracy and administrative functions. Several centuries of Ottoman rule had created an overlay of self-rule as a concept of co-existence. The millet system had delivered in its own way. Now, this could very well be seen as a cynical way to prolong an empire by allowing for some autonomy, so as to perpetuate the larger goals of the empire. Overall, breaking bread meant sharing the space and the peace, and the opposite was not really in the cards. Except of course my grandfather and his small band of law-and-order hoodlums, who kept alive a nasty turmoil, like an underground river from hell. Most of his followers were younger people.

As the War came to an end, the concept of shared space had become quite prevalent. Markets, pilgrimage sites, museums, parks and open amphitheatres were shared spaces. People from different religions converged there or walked by each other. There was no obvious animosity. But, as I came to understand, shared *spaces* were not shared *places*. Irrespective of how attempts were made to allow autonomy for various religious communities, it did not really lead to people living together, right away. They went back to their communities, as night fell.

But when the partisans had their time in power, citizens felt they had solved many of their differences. Religion and ethnicity went on the back burner and folks even started sharing places! They intermarried and learnt to chat in each other's languages. They joked and cried together.

As the partisan generation faded away, the young—who were the same age as me—got too restless to carry on the carefully attenuated equilibrium. The old hatreds and distrusts crawled to the surface with some energy. And there was very little presence of mind in the population to contain this revival of religious nationalisms. Suspicion, hatred and the historic mistrust rose to the surface.

***

By the time the two old men with the wrinkled faces had departed, two young men had taken over their spaces. One wore a leather jacket, with large zippers. The other wore a pin-striped jacket and baggy pants. The one with the leather jacket wore a very stylish bowler and the other had his hair greased well enough that a strong wind had no impact. The one with the bowler put his hat down on a seat. Their foreheads were smooth. As they spoke, cigarettes dangled out of their mouths.

My time had come to leave Sabzic.

My mama closed the door of the house before I climbed into the taxi that would take me to the train station. I rolled down the window to see if she would look out through the bathroom window, as I would when I observed my grandfather, years ago. She did not seem to be there.

I looked away and stared at the bus stop, where Nika's skirt would billow, as the warm wind blew on a late summer's day. The walls of the compound were still intact. Chipped plaster still showed the remnants of the paintings that my grandfather's followers had once tried to please him with. The rupture was sad and necessary.

On April 4, 1949, the foreign ministers of 12 countries in North America and Western Europe gathered in Washington,

DC, to sign the North Atlantic Treaty. It was primarily a security pact, with Article 5 stating that a military attack against any of the signatories would be considered an attack against them all. I was only nineteen and I realized that the War did not end as well as popular conceptions made it out to be.

Chapter Twenty-Nine

On December 22, 1954, two world leaders, met in New Delhi and explained the non-alignment movement. Nehru and Tito in a joint statement said "the policy of non-alignment adopted and pursued by their respective countries is not 'neutrality' or 'neutralism' and therefore passivity, as sometimes alleged, but is a positive, active and constructive policy seeking to lead to collective peace."

It was cold outside. Unusual for Zurich. My wife and I sat down at a coffee shop. She had finished teaching a semester in the University and was expecting her contract position to evolve further. The windows of the café were being cleaned by a young Indian man with a turban. We were seeing more Indians appearing all over Europe, doing the hard and low-paying jobs. He was spraying an obnoxious amount of glass-cleaner on the panes and cleaning them with paper towels. He was following instructions, no doubt. But the overpowering smell of the ammonia and alcohol was drifting towards our table. I looked at him with a "really?" look. And he smiled and walked away and let loose another cloud of spray, further away from us. I went back to the magazine, while my wife was reading the newspaper.

Nineteen eighty-five was being discussed as the year of the spy in various European journals. I was shocked to find out that while Gorbachev was busy bringing about change, as he saw it, in the Soviet Union, at least seven US citizens were arrested for carrying out espionage activities on behalf of Israel, Soviet Union and in one case China. None of those arrested were really of the Rosenberg variety. In other words, they were not atomic scientists, or guidance system specialists, who felt that helping out the Soviet Union was a moral duty. They were mostly thieves. Stealing equipment, special switches for detonation and supplying them to these countries in exchange for large sums of gratuity. Some of them had led criminal lives in the past and some were hapless gamblers and drunkards. Most were caught in sting operations by the FBI or CIA and either got light sentences commuted or hung themselves in cells. Remarkably different from Julius and Ethel Rosenberg. I was engrossed in reading their legal positions of defence, in a glossy German magazine.

As I sipped my coffee, my wife suddenly straightened herself, sat upright and passed a news item to me from the newspaper she was reading. I looked at her. I could not see her eyes, as she wore very large brown sunglasses.

"Look! This is in Sabzic!"

I took the paper from her and started reading. When I was growing up there, the word "Turks" was not much in use. Yes, we heard it occasionally. It was a pejorative term for Muslims. The headline said that a mob had been marching through the town routinely, with torches and hurling abuses at "Turks." Some mosques had been set on fire and nasty graffiti had appeared in the very plaza where my grandfather had tried to whip a band of his followers into a frenzy. This time, they were in smart designer jeans, gold plated crosses bobbing on their chests. They were young and middle aged, men and women. Their faces contorted as they were photographed crossing the bridge again! Even after four hundred years, the bridge was providing passage to malice and hatred. The news report said that an elderly person of Muslim origin was chased down the Strand and beaten up very badly. He was left unconscious. Another one had managed to flee by jumping into the canal and swimming across. It was not clear from the report if there were fatalities, but black smoke had been rising from various parts of the city and several mosques and a Jewish cemetery had been vandalized. The local police stood by and allowed the mob to go on a rampage for several hours. Sabzic, said the report, was becoming notorious as a hotbed for this type of violence.

When I got home, I would call my Mama. She was in her early eighties. We spoke often on the phone, but I had not visited her for nearly two years or even more perhaps. My wife said we should go home and call her right away.

Sometimes, the report suggested, pogroms were being conducted and houses were being identified that had Muslim residents. One ethnicity and religion was bent on chasing out another religion and ethnicity. It was quite simple. There was no real record of past conviviality left. That torch had not been passed on. Or, maybe it was that memory of that past that was not considered relevant. The reporter lamented that the elderly were not that visible, compared to a previous visit that she had made some ten years back. The coffee was not poured from a height and made to froth and fancy gleaming Italian machines provided the coffee for the young and the old alike. Things happened so fast that

231

everyone moved on to new issues and had no time for the past and how things had unfolded during and after the War.

As I read further, the newspaper said that some bodies had been found floating in the canal.

I had received a letter from my mother a week ago.

Dearest Ben, Hope you and Hita are doing well. And Jonah is growing as fast as he can. Because the more you stay a child, as you know, the less the world will care for your ideas. It is a child's ideas and questions that unravel the most. But children are made expendable, till they make or bring money home. Or, you could be a peasant child and you work in the field for your parents. You get two meals a day and get to stare at the girls who stand by the fence in the next farm, when the sun sets.

Even the collectives seem to be falling apart.

I hope Jonah does not require a tutor! That was a poor joke! But as you surely know, Shaf meant a lot to all of us. Hope you can find him someday. My health is not bad. I read a lot and I write! In a diary! Someday you will get to read. No, it is not about Magnetism! It is about cooking bad food for myself on Saturdays! Who will I cook for? You remember Ana? The woman who looked after that wretched grandfather of yours, Marcus. One day she came over with a stew when Marcus was gone, when you were still a kid. She told me that one night he came over to her room and started touching her. When she moved away towards the wall, he grabbed her and tried to get on top of her, calling her a Romani slut! Well, it turns out that after his death, one of his assistants inherited his little mansion and after this impudent fellow moved in with his family, they threw Ana out. She spent a lot of time with me chatting and we cooked together, when the estate had not yet been settled. It turns out that she was selling jewellery from a cart in the Strand. Well! Her body was found last week, bloated and stuck under some branches in the canal. Her throat had been slit. Many from the old days seemed to know her and also because of the jewellery she sold. Ben, this is not the world your Bo fought for. Think about it! What does it take to unlearn and forget? Nothing really. And now I hear that they will be revising the courses being taught in schools.

The carpet looked good from a distance. But, when you put your nose to it, it smells.

I wish you all a good summer.

Take good care, your mama!

I remembered the Romani, who would walk by at odd hours, appearing from nowhere, mumbling, "dusk to dawn, dusk to dawn." I did not understand what he meant. I found a Romani idiom that said that *daylight hides evil and the night brings out the devil.* That between sunset and sunrise, all that you had achieved during the day, would be undone, if you were not up, as well, at night.

It seemed a campaign had started. A campaign that would negate the green-blue serenity that flowed through our state of mind; that what we had come to know as our town, our canal and the bridge that crossed over, was not ours any longer. And now a campaign was on to make it into a red-brown nightmare. I knew that this could not be averted. The bridge would not last. We got up and left.

Our son, Jonah, would be home from school, riding his bike that I had just bought for him.

Section Four

Jonah, The Serf and the Remington

Chapter Thirty

It was February 27, 1985. On this day, the Government of Poland ordered the expulsion of the US Military Attaché in Warsaw, Col. Frederick Myers and his wife Barbara, for taking photographs of a military installation in a small town outside Warsaw. They were ordered to take a commercial flight out to Zurich, immediately. The tit-for-tat measures in the dying days of the Cold War had begun and one-time actor and now president, Ronald Reagan, announced that within 48 hours the Polish Military Attaché at Washington, DC was to leave the country, as well.

I had been working on my homework from my Coordinated Science Program teacher. He had casually asked us as to why we did not fall through the floor when we were sitting in our second-floor classroom. Can we explain it with some detailed numbers or concepts? Of course, some of my classmates thought it was a rather silly question. How could our bodies break through the wooden floor, with beams underneath and drop to the ground floor? We were to come back the next day with the answers. I had found a notebook in my father's office, where the same question had been answered by a tutor of his some forty years back. It was composed of diagrams of electrons with arrows projecting away from the sole of boots, and confronting a cross-sectional sketch of a floor which also had arrows projecting up towards the boots. I knew the answer. But what really amazed me was that my classmates were extraordinarily lazy. We had just finished a whole course on the interaction of gravity and electromagnetic force. Our teacher had clearly stated that these were the two strong forces, but there were other forces, both weak and strong that existed in the subatomic level and as well in the universe. In that notebook in my father's office, there were sketches that clearly indicated that electrons, though identical, did not like each other. At the bottom of our shoe, electrons would be repelling the electrons on the surface of the floor and this repulsion would counteract the forces of gravity.

My father was talking on the phone, continuously, and breaking up my concentration. My mother had stepped out for a while. I went into my father's office and took the notebook to my desk. He allowed me such liberties. And besides, he was engrossed in a long-distance conversation and would not have noticed me.

A few days later, my father left on a rather complicated trip. He was taking a flight to Munich and then he would be renting a car and driving to the city he was born in. The city was called Sabzic. That is what I had gathered. It seemed like he was in a rush. It would take him more than a day to reach there by train and so he was on the phone for a long time with an agent, before he decided he would catch a plane, and then he would rent a car outside Munich and drive for another eleven hours. He seemed quite excited and yet pretty tense. I did not understand why he was making such a tortuous trip. He could have flown. Perhaps he needed some time to reflect as he drove.

On March 11, this year, 1985 that is, a fellow named Mikhail Gorbachev had just been declared the new chief of the Soviet Communists, the day before. At the age of 54, he was elected to the General Secretariat by their Politburo. I remember this guy, with the birthmarks on his forehead— they looked like paint peeling off a rusting white helmet because he introduced two words in our history class. Glasnost and Perestroika.

***

My name is Jonah. It is a Hebrew name, just in case you were wondering. My father is a lawyer, who loves chocolates. He has them in a big jar in his office, which I have visited several times. He also has them in another jar in our kitchen. My mother's name is Hita, but her real name is Anahita. She is from Persia, also known as Iran. She is an artist. They met in Teheran, where my father had gone to visit a client. He has been to Iran many times, but once he met her, he did not go back again. I think it was 1969 that he stopped going. And my mother came to live with him in Zurich and voila! I was born there in 1970. At least, that is what I am aware of.

***

A few weeks ago, a man appeared at our door. He was short and elderly. Probably ten years older than my father. He wore a baggy pair of trousers. And a mismatched tweed jacket, with square designs on it. His nose hairs were quite visible on his upper lips, almost like two juniper bushes were pushing out of his nostrils. He wore a brown beret that was not well placed on his head. His hair was cut short around his ears, and as a result they looked rather large. His shoulders sloped down and he had a very kind look on his face. He removed his beret and I noticed that he had a large bald patch on his head and his forehead was polished and without any wrinkles. He was there for about one and a half hours. My parents brought pastries, chocolates from a confectionary, a block away from our house. He had the coffee and did not have much else. He did nibble at some chocolates. He had called my father a week before. And I heard the whole conversation. My father had kept asking him the same questions on the phone, over and over again.

"I remember you, very well. Yes, yes of course! I even recognize your voice. But, how can you be sure, it is him?"

Then the man said something and my father kept repeating.

"How can I feel assured? And how are you so sure? Yes, please do come. I am looking forward."

I heard everything and I was pretty sure that it excited my father so much that he went into the bathroom and sat on the toilet for quite a while after that phone call. He has done that in the past when he was tense.

I asked my father, who was the guy that had called.

"You will see him next week." So, when the time came and the bell rang at the door, I rushed to open it.

The man entered with a large bag on his shoulder. I did not like that, but I was quite intrigued and interested in what my father had arranged with such anxiety. The man asked for Monsieur Ben.

"Yes, we have been waiting for you." I answered with the voice of an adult. I was just about fifteen.

The sun had nearly set and while we had large windows, the glow of a Zurich sunset cast long shadows in the room. I asked him to take a seat. A chandelier above our dining table, moved gently, without making any sounds and my mother walked in. I could see his eyes in the glare and while he had walked in wearing a pair of glasses, when he took them off, I realized his eyes were resting in deep hollow pockets. He rose up to greet her. He spoke in French to my mother.

My father walked in and shook his hand, holding both hands together.

As he was obviously trying to figure him out, my father kept staring at him. I was quite embarrassed by this silent invigilation. The man, fortunately, had his eyes focused on the coffee. He did not seem to want to look up. He was a quiet man. He seemed to be carrying out a duty, he had been assigned.

"Are you staying in the city?"

"No, Mr. Ben," he said, "I won't stay too long."

"Ah! So, will you go back to Sabzic?"

"No, Mr. Ben. I have moved out." He was clearly economic with his answers. My father caught on and did not ask any further questions.

"I have come to visit you, after I found out about your whereabouts."

"Ah! I am curious, as to how you found out where I lived."

"A year ago, I had gone to return this bag to your mother. She did not want it. She was very happy to see me. She told me that you lived in Zurich. And through some contacts..."

"Ah! My father's old comrades, I suppose?"

"Yes," he said, with some hesitation as to how my father would react. "The ones who fought and built our nation... That is right." He continued, "It is your father who had asked that I find a way to deliver it to you, after the War was over."

My father smiled.

"That was forty years ago!" He seemed sad. They were both sitting across from each other. But I could see that the stranger with the bag was looking at my father earnestly. And my father seemed deeply blue. He stared down at the coffee table.

"Yes, I know. I had to recover something, that was lost for all these years. I had to trace it back. I found it finally and I must keep my promise to your Bo. So, I am here! But we fought a good fight!"

After a while, my father muttered on.

"Yes! Yes! I know what you are saying. But unfortunately, they constructed a nation based on their beliefs, but not the reality on the ground, right?"

"Some say that...but so far it is still working, is it not?"

"Not for long! I had also thought that we could live together. It was a daydream. The animosities run deep. It is a tinderbox, waiting for someone to strike the flint. Everyone has their own militias, don't they?"

"I wish we could be left alone by all the powers, to solve our problems ourselves."

"True, but that will not happen. They will never let that experiment go on. Besides, we are all tribes, ultimately. We hid behind a good idea of confederation."

My father sounded like a statesman. "We fought a good fight against the fascists. And you did! Meanwhile, there are powers who do not care much about such ideas. The partisan generation is gone. Memories will soon be wiped clean."

"Do you really think it is that bad?"

"Well! The business of rotating the president does not work. We believed we had buried all our differences, our languages, our religions—but really, not so. The toxins are running deep in the river. Some of us feel that some amongst us got the bigger share of the pie; others felt they should not be less important as they were the biggest population. Some of us built bridges, others are ready to bomb them. So, the animosities have all come to the surface. Muslims were hated before and now they are hated even more. That does not help, does it? After all they fought together with us. Don't you think so?"

"You know better, Mr. Ben! But I think you may be right. You have studied all this. I saw you when you were a young boy only!"

He took a sip of his coffee. Then he took a piece of paper from his jacket pocket, unfolded it and gave it to my father.

"That is the address. With some instructions. As we discussed on the phone." He said that quite firmly.

"He may need some help. Maybe he needs to be taken out from that hole he has chosen to live in."

My father looked at it carefully. There were detailed instructions as to how to reach the address. Then he looked up at the man. My father put the piece of paper down on the coffee table. I noticed that there was a name written on the reverse side. My father had not noticed it. Shafic Pašalić.

"I know this area. It has changed. It will not be difficult. But you said he is not in good shape. Is he ill?"

"That is what a lot of people thought about him. But I did not think so. He was always a few years ahead of his friends and family. He had ideas about the future and sometimes he lived in the future and it clashed with the present. So, he was branded as either an extremist or a lunatic. He is neither. But he is tough..."

"Yes...as nails. And what is in that bag?" My father finally took notice.

"Well, let me open it for you." Having said that, he picked up the bag which he had left by our doorstep. It was

243

quite heavy, from the way he lifted it up and put it down at his feet. He then opened the zipper. The sound was like a carcass had been opened with a buck knife. He then put his hand in and slowly pulled out a double barrel shot gun and held it up. The setting sun sent its rays to bounce off the barrel and I winced.

The word Remington was embossed on the side of the barrel, on one side. I peered over to look at it. My mother turned away. He handed it to my father and my Bo hesitated to touch it. His eyes were watery. Then he stood up, holding it. My mother turned back again. She seemed to know what it was all about. I had no idea.

My father stared at the shiny barrel and hammers. His eyes glistened.

"I have not asked you, your name." My Bo looked up at him, the tears had started coming down his cheeks.

"Serf. The Serf. Let it remain that."

Having said that he took the gun from my Bo, put it back in the bag and laid it down on the floor, waved his hand, turned around and left.

My father stared at the door as it shut slowly on its own.

"The Remington is back," my father said. My mother stood staring at the door, as my father lifted the bag up and looked at her and then he put his arms around me.

END

Acknowledgements

How It All Began

I am told that acknowledgements are something that readers always steal a look at before they start reading the novel. And therefore, I shall start with a few important ideas right here.

When I was growing up in a newly post-colonial world, where Asia, Africa and Latin America had tossed out the foreign occupiers of their lands for the most part, there was also the concept of maintaining equidistance from super-power nations. One of the nations that upheld this equidistance was Yugoslavia. Yugoslavia was unique because Muslims, Jews, Catholics, Orthodox and others had come out of their Partisan resistance to Fascism and Nazism, and emerged as a model for a people living, interacting and growing together. Religious nationalism did not define the country. My father, Amiya Kumar Bose, a cardiologist, was impressed by Tito's Yugoslavia. About 134 non-aligned nations eventually happily chose to follow the direction of countries like Yugoslavia, India, Egypt, Indonesia, Ghana and a few others. So, the question is why did Yugoslavia fall apart in April of 1992? Was it because of the relentless, savage bombing of the country by NATO for 78 days? Was there also a deeper malaise of religion-bound ethnic nationalism, which lay festering under the warm blanket of a comfortable secular nation? Was it possible for people from different religious backgrounds to intermarry and create a blend of people who can live together? I owe it to my late father for germinating some of these ideas, which transcend concepts like *laïcité* which are in vogue today.

There is something else that has for a long time either stoked my curiosity or paralyzed my sanity—the relationship between Physics and human behaviour. If there are only four forces in the world—gravity, electromagnetic and strong and weak subatomic forces, and if the theory of everything encompasses everything, then why is there no parity or a sense of balance in human behaviour? After all, we are composed of nothing but perhaps a billion subatomic particles or forces. Is the bending of the space-time curve and the subatomic forces within us, reason enough for us not to go into fits of madness and behave nastily towards each other? But then there is the birth of capital as a vile motivating force.

I would like to thank Robin Philpot, my publisher with whom I have had several energizing discussions during the editing and publishing of my previous novel, *Fog*, and with this one as well. I would also like to thank Blossom Thom, poet, writer and eloquent observer of the world we live in, for editing this novel. Then there is Françoise Miquet, a gentle, thoughtful and very informed friend (about West Asia and the Balkans), who fed me with significant documents and books during my one and a half years of research on the area and the Ottoman era. I would be remiss if I did not mention my close friends and colleagues at *montrealserai. com* who have been very supportive of all my adventures in writing, agitating and as well restraining me for my unnecessary enthusiasm for quelling banality and triteness in what we see, read and hear. My friend Nilambri Ghai, a founding editor at Montreal Serai has always been a source of critical appreciation of my work. I would like to thank Sherry Simon, a friend at a writers' group I have belonged to, for more than two decades. She observes urban cultures, through translation, in transition and has been very supportive of this novel.

If folks have made it to this point, either by reading the novel or reading this segment first, I would like them to know that I would not have made it through these last four years without the love, care and detailed observations of Lisa, my life partner, and my walking buddy and frequent interlocutor Willis.

Printed by Imprimerie Gauvin
Gatineau, Québec